A Creepy Company

YEARLING BOOKS/YOUNG YEARLINGS/YEARLING CLASSICS are designed especially to entertain and enlighten young people. Patricia Reilly Giff, consultant to this series, received her bachelor's degree from Marymount College and a master's degree in history from St. John's University. She holds a Professional Diploma in Reading and a Doctorate of Humane Letters from Hofstra University. She was a teacher and reading consultant for many years, and is the author of numerous books for young readers.

For a complete listing of all Yearling titles, write to
Dell Readers Service,
P.O. Box 1045,
South Holland, IL 60473.

A Creepy Company

Ten Tales of Terror

Joan Aiken

A Yearling Book

Published by
Bantam Doubleday Dell Books for Young Readers
a division of
Bantam Doubleday Dell Publishing Group, Inc.
1540 Broadway
New York, New York 10036

ISBN: 0-440-40993-4

Printed in the United States of America
February 1995
10 9 8 7 6 5 4 3 2 1

To Richard Dalby

Contents

Dead Man's Lane

If you run hot water over the top of the whistling kettle, it lets out a howl, did you know that? I always do it when I go to my father's house, he has a whistler, and young Andy, my half-brother, he's only five, he always says, "*Don't*, Sam! Don't *do* that! You're hurting it!" Which makes me laugh.

Matter of fact, I don't go to my father's house a lot. We haven't much to say to each other. He moved last year—with my stepmother and the twins—out to this small country town, Crowbridge. It's an hour on the bike to get there. It's true he gave me the bike so that I could. And now he's promised to take me to Paris for a week, but only if I pass my exams. Which are coming up in a couple of weeks. So . . .

No problem about the exams, mind you. None that I can see. I don't know why Dad gets into such a fuss. He wrote me a letter saying he'd heard from the Old Swine that I wasn't doing as well in class as I should. Should!

Who the hell is going to lay down the law about how well I should do?

Anyway, I'll be perfectly OK. Apart from anything else, I know this guy who can sell you a pen that guarantees you pass. And as well as the pen—which costs a fair slice, I will admit, but I'm going to ask Dad for an advance on my summer quarter's allowance—as well as the pen, the guy has this stuff. And the stuff is truly, truly five-dimensional. Gives you a lift right out of your own mind into something a hundred percent higher and faster. The Great Chief Mind, maybe.

So—like I say—I don't go to Dad's place all that often anymore.

When I do go, Ann, that's my stepmother, always gives me a great big hello, welcome on the mat, all that, but I reckon it can't be very sincere. Why should she be pleased to see me, anyway? I'm not hers, after all, she's got two of her own, even if one of them is a bit non-functioning. She's got no call to welcome me, and I don't trust it. If there is one thing I can't stand, it's falseness. Ann said once, "Your father misses you. I'm glad for *his* sake."

Well, I ask you? What can you make of that?

Last time I went to Crowbridge was a few weeks ago, to pick up some of my tapes that were still there. It's true, the kids always seem pleased enough to see me, they hug my legs; but then I reckon anybody coming to the house is a treat to them. Young Kate will always be the way she is now, she can't develop anymore, there's some long medical explanation for that; Ann and my dad say it won't make any difference, she's one of the family whether she develops or not.

2

Easy to say that *now;* they may think differently in twenty years' time. The one it's rough on, in my view, is young Andy; he don't know what's ahead of him. Anyway—none of my business. But, for that reason, they don't have a lot of visitors coming to the house. People fight shy. You know.

Well, I went down to pick up my tapes. The way you get to Dad's place in Ferry Road, Crowbridge, there's a really crafty shortcut. Gives me a terrific feeling every time I use it.

As you get to the town, the main road from Galhampton turns left at the bridge, and then you have to circle right round Crowbridge on the perimeter road, across a pair of rotaries, and then back into Warden Street. It's all a one-way system.

Whereas, if you take the cut down Dead Man's Lane, you are there in a jiffy.

It was Ann who first showed me the shortcut; she's lived in the town before, see, and knows all its crannies like the palm of her hand. As you come down the hill, Pelican Hill it's called, named from the pub up at the top, you have to watch out very, very sharply, because it's a little, inconspicuous turn, looks more like somebody's private driveway than a public road. And in fact there are two private driveways before you come to it, so you have to watch for the third entry, which is Dead Man's Lane. Why it's called Dead Man's Lane I don't know, and Ann doesn't know either. Some dead man long, long ago. Whatever he did, or what happened to him, must have been pretty impressive, for the lane to be called after him. It's queer that nobody seems to remember. The lane isn't at all long, maybe a quarter of a mile, and halfway along there's an acute left-hand bend. Lord help you if you meet somebody coming the other way, for—would you believe it—they've never made Dead Man's Lane into a one-way road, I suppose because so very few people actually know and use it. At the bottom end it turns into Rope Walk, and *that* leads into Warden Street, where you only have to turn right and there you are in Ferry Road. Saves all that circuit round the town.

But the thing is, you have to be really sharp, coming down Pelican Hill, to judge your moment and slip across in front of the opposing traffic, into that tiny little deep-cut entrance. It always gives me a terrific zing when I do it on the bike—one minute you are chugging down the main road, among the heavy traffic, buses, trucks going to the harbor, hundreds of tourist cars, then—zwoosh!—you are out of it all, zipping down between those high narrow banks, with close-packed trees and bushes making a tunnel of it, thick and dark, arching over your head. Round the sharp left-hand bend, holding your breath in case there's something on the other side coming toward you—which, up to now, there never *has* been—and then, like coming out of a tube, you are back in bright daylight, rolling into Rope Walk, which has little red-brick Victorian cottages on one side, with box-sized front gardens. On the other side there's old timbered storehouses and a car park. The whole trip along Dead Man's Lane takes only a couple of minutes—less, maybe—but there's a kind of fierce thrill about it—like surf-riding, or swallowing an oyster, or the Big Wheel.

I lie awake at night, sometimes, thinking about it.

Funny, though—it's not *possible* to lie awake thinking about it for more than a moment or two: it always puts you to sleep. Better than counting sheep! The one really surefire soporific; it works every, every time. I've sometimes thought it should be possible to patent it, to those guys who do operations without anesthesia, by hypnotizing their patients; you get an awkward one who won't respond to hypnosis, you just take him down Dead Man's Lane a couple of times and then get him to go into recall. Of course he'd have to be able to ride a bike, that's one problem.

Well, the last time I went to Dad's house was a bit of a frost. Why, I still am not quite sure. I got there, Dad wasn't in yet, he took some dreary job, teaching at the local Middle School. Had to get what he could, as they wanted to live in the town. And he was off organizing a botanical excursion, wouldn't be in for a couple of hours, though it was a Saturday.

I'm never going to get married. I just don't see all this adapting your lifestyle and habits to suit another person, because they want to live in a place. I'm going to set myself up in one room with all my electronic equipment—as soon as I'm able—and that will be that. Then I'll do what I want.

Anyway, I walked into the house in Ferry Road and the twins each came and grabbed a leg; then, after a while, Kate crawled off, in her dopey way, but Andy followed me wherever I went. He can talk the hind leg off a mackerel, that one.

I was hunting for my tapes and, of course, they'd all been *put away*. I had a hideous job finding them, had to shift half the furniture in the downstairs rooms to get at them in the cupboards where they had been stowed. There's a million cupboards in that house—I reckon that's why Ann likes it so, she's got what I'd call an obsessionally tidy nature, she can't stand to see things lying about in the open; when the kids have finished playing, every block has to go back into its box, trucks into their garage, crayons into the tin, paint water emptied, paper stacked together—it's enough to give the kids hang-ups that'll last into their nineties, if you ask *me*. Which nobody does. Of course maybe when you are in your nineties you prefer to have the ballpoints all sorted into their separate colors. I wouldn't know.

Anyway Andy helped me shift the big couch, and the chests and other things so as to get at my tapes—he loved that, he thought it was a great game to drag all the furniture into different places. And I made a heap of the tapes, for Dad had said he'd put the bike on the car roof-rack and drive me back that night.

Ann had gone off round the corner to the little Good-Buy Supermarket, which is all they have there; she said it was a good chance for her to go out while I was there to baby-sit, and she'd get her hair done at the same time.

Luckily Kate had fallen into one of her endless naps. I'd really hate to have to be responsible for *her*. Andy's no problem, I'll say that for him. He just chats along.

When I'd got the tapes sorted out I was hungry—hadn't had any breakfast before I started out from Mum's—so I went and took a look in the fridge. Got out some pizzas and some chops and some other things that were there, and stuck them in the microwave. And ate the lot. Plus a big tub of butter-candy ice cream, and a cake and some ginger buns that I found in the pantry. Moving all that furniture about had really hollowed me out. I asked Andy if he wanted any, but he said no, they'd only just had their lunch when I got there. At two o'clock! I ask you!

Then I remembered I wanted to make some shelves for my bedroom back at Mum's, so I went into Dad's workshop and found a couple of boards, and brought them into the kitchen, where it was warmer—I don't know how Dad can stand that cold workroom of his—and sawed them up. Andy loved watching that. He wanted to try sawing, but of course I wouldn't let him. But I let him play with the sawdust. He made it into patterns on the carpet.

While I worked, I was telling him about coming down Dead Man's Lane.

"*I* know Dead Man's Lane," says Andy, "we go that way when Mum takes us to the Bluebell Woods. Up Dead Man's Lane, up Pelican Hill. At my school they sing a song about Dead Man's Lane."

Andy goes to school, though he's only five. Kate doesn't, of course, and never will. But I reckon Ann is glad to get one of them off her hands for a few hours.

"What's the song?" I say to Andy, thinking maybe it'll explain the name.

He sings:

"Dead Man, Dead Man, in Dead Man's Lane,
Tell me once, tell me again,
Tell me all I want to know,
I'll be your friend if you do so.

7

A CREEPY COMPANY

Three times, three times round
Drive three times round the town
Then down Dead Man's Lane you go
And he'll tell you all you want to know."

The tune, sung in Andy's droning little voice, was a bit like Baa Baa Black Sheep. I get him to sing it again, then I join in, and we have a real good time. Kate never wakes.

In the middle, Dad comes back. I suppose by now it's about half past five. He seems a bit annoyed—what about, I can't make out—and then Ann comes back, and he lights into her because tea isn't ready. Ann's your silent sort, she never says anything, just puts on a kettle—it boils right away, and screams like a banshee because I'd had it on, just before, to make a big jug of coffee and chocolate mixed.

"I'll just go out for a few things," Ann tells Dad, looking rattled, and out she goes again. Dad stumps about—spreading sawdust everywhere—and says nothing either.

So I listen to a few of my tapes till Ann gets back, and then Dad says, "While she's making a meal, I'll take you back." That surprises me, as I thought I was to spend the evening there, but, OK, I collect my stuff and take it out to the Escort.

Kate's still asleep, but I say goodbye to Andy—Ann's in the kitchen frying chops, she gives me a kind of wave with her face turned away over the stove—and then we slam off in Dad's car with my bike on the roof. And he gives me this long saga about working harder at school.

I don't listen to him much because I know perfectly

well that I'm going to be all right. I'm absolutely sure of that. I do remember, though, to get the extra quarter's allowance out of him, though he's pretty glum and surly about it.

"What do you want it for?"

I owe a couple of the fellows, I tell him, and he's glum about that too.

"And when you do come down here—I wish you'd be more considerate to Ann—"

That really knocks me. "What did I do wrong, for Sam's sake?"

He just shrugs. And I begin to think the trip to Paris is off. But no, he still refers to it. Only if I pass the exams. And he wants me to come down to Crowbridge the week before. "That way," he says, "you can get some studying done in peace without all those friends of yours hanging around."

Well, OK; I don't argue. By then I'll have got the special pen—warranted to work, never fails—and some more of the stuff, the powder. Power powder, they call it. You sniff it—a little, but not too much, specially before a bike ride. Never too much.

So I say goodbye to Dad, and he drives off at top speed, as soon as I have my things out of the car, because he's always dead scared of running into Mum.

He seems a bit sad. I never know what he's thinking.

And that night, when I go to bed, I remember Andy's little rhyme: "Dead Man, Dead Man, in Dead Man's Lane . . ." and I say it over and I'm off to sleep as quick as blowing out a match.

A CREEPY COMPANY

So now it's the week before the exams, and I'm on my way back to Crowbridge. A dull, rainy afternoon. And, as I come to the top of Pelican Hill, I remember the rhyme again. "Three times, three times round, Drive three times round the town. . . ."

Just for laughs, I think, I'll *do* that. Three times round the circuit of the perimeter road—it'll be a game to see how fast I can get round Crowbridge, I'll check the speed on my digital radio—up the hill again, round the rotary at the top, then, zing! back down the hill, and into Dead Man's Lane.

So that's what I do.

First circuit takes four and a half minutes; by the second I've cut it to four. Third, in slightly under four, I'm really getting the feel of it now. Up the hill in a rainy streak, round by the old Pelican pub—then down again, with the air cutting away from me in bow-waves that you can almost *see*.

Across in front of the traffic—there's some braking and skidding, but not from *my* front wheel, which clips neatly in between the high entrance-banks of Dead Man's Lane—and now we're hurtling, we're zooming down the green tunnel, through the smell of wet green leaves and mud.

And now we come to the left-hand bend—and round beyond it I believe the Dead Man is waiting, waiting to tell me all I want to know. . . .

My Disability

Well, my dear, at first we couldn't even get *on* to the boat, because those fools of organizers hadn't seen fit to check on the one-way streets in Stjøck, or whatever the name of the godforsaken port is—Stjøck was the word, I can tell you, there we sat, in our coaches, at ten in the evening, for three-quarters of an hour, if you'll believe me, while they went to request permission from the harbormaster to take us down a hundred yards to the dockside. Permission refused. I was obliged to give Herbert a piece of my mind, as I had packed some biscuits and a flask of tea in my on-plane bag, but dear Herbert, just like him, had put that bag with the other things in the coach luggage-hold, and of course we were not allowed to get out. Too much traffic in the street. And then, my dear, the coaches had to back up the hill and go a long way round, and we had to *walk*, half a mile at least, in the snow, for it was snowing, along the dockside, climbing over and around every kind of rope and barrel and crate and capstan, or whatever name they give those things. Imagine! And me with my disability, you can figure for yourself how I felt.

So then, at long last, we came to our ship, the *Queen of the Fjord*, ha ha, and I can tell you she didn't look much in the dark.

There were a couple of girls, they can't have been more than eighteen, welcoming us on board. Herbert gave them the glad eye, naturally.

"The wine will soon be open," they kept saying. "Join us in the bar. We are just getting the wine off the ice now."

"It would be more to the point," I told Herbert, "if they put a kettle on the gas for a nice cup of tea or coffee."

"Well, you've got that flask you kept asking for on the bus," he said—most unreasonably.

"My dear Herbert," I said, "you can't expect me to drink that *now*; it will be cold by this time." Which it was.

First of all we went to find our cabin. My dear, it was no bigger than a dog kennel. Not a single hook to hang our coats on. Only two coat hangers in a wardrobe the size of a golf bag. One forty-watt bulb in the middle of the ceiling and, of course, the bedside lights did not work. No drawers; nowhere to keep my sewing kit—let alone underwear and Herbert's socks. "You'll have to get the cabin steward to bring us some more hangers and see to those lights," I told Herbert.

"Let's go up to the bar first," he said—like a man; so, naturally, I said no more.

Up we went, and, though they had a few bottles and

were opening them, need you ask, my dear, it was only *red* wine. Poison to me, as you know. "You'll have to make them get some white," I told Herbert. But he only said, "All in good time. Have mineral water for now." He was busy chatting up the bar steward and the two hostesses, both blondes, who were passing round sandwiches. Not proper sandwiches, needless to say—they were that open-topped kind the Scandinavians go in for, with olives and prawns and bits of fruit rolling off the ham and cheese in every direction; a thoroughly messy way of eating, I call it. Specially standing up. Smorgasbord? More like *over*board. Bits were being squashed underfoot wherever you looked. We went off to bed very soon.

Breakfast was continental and did not impress us. I'd had a bad night. I hate feather comforters: either you are too hot and suffocate, or the thing falls off and you freeze to death.

Plainly they were not used to people asking for tea, though they did produce it in the end, with an ill grace. (And—after a day or two, mark you—they found a box of cornflakes for Herbert.)

We had set sail overnight—another black mark for the management, since we never did manage to get a look at the town where we embarked—and were already steaming up this fjord, Skripsøfjord, or something. I must say, my dear, that fjords leave me cold, absolutely cold. See one, you've seen them all. Steep, bleak sides, sweeping down into the black water at an angle that gives you toothache, mountain peaks so high above that you get a stiff neck craning up to look at them. Trees, what there are, nothing but evergreens and those scrubby little larches; every now and then some great bird goes flapping overhead or suddenly smacks down into the water after a fish.

Fish! Don't speak to me of fish. We had it at every meal—smoked fish, pickled fish, dried fish, baked fish, fried fish. *Eel*. Have you ever eaten eel, my dear? *Don't start*.

On the first day we met our three guides, who would be looking after us on boat excursions, or coach trips ashore (in the parts where there were *roads*, that is).

My dear, two of the guides were *girls*, called Anni and Christa, both blondes. "We'd better pick the man," I told Herbert. "A man would be more use if anything went wrong." So we picked Jürgen—or Yurg, as everybody called him. He was a big, hefty, red-faced fellow, with a pale-yellow thatch of hair. Almost white it was really, looked odd above his red shiny face. But he was full of jokes, always a laugh, always chatting up the lady passengers—widows, mostly, there were more women than men. But Yurg had his jokes with the men, too—mostly over an aquavit in the bar.

"So: we go to look for the lost island," he told Herbert one day. "That will be our goal on this trip."

"Lost island, what lost island?" said Herbert. "No one told *me* about any lost island. I thought it was all ornithology and archaeology."

"Ach, only my joke. It is a folktale, a legend. Up at the head of Skripsøfjord, seventy miles from the sea, is an island where Trolls inhabit."

"*Trolls?*"

"They fly through the air, so goes the legend, carrying bundles of logs," said Yurg. "And they have power to

14

change their shape. But mostly their shape is to have three heads, and blue scales, and to give off cold, as a furnace gives off heat. And they hate all noise, that is the only thing that annoys them."

There was a little boy, Ollie, on board, who happened to be in the bar just then, sitting with his parents, Professor and Mrs. Kendrick, drinking orange juice and listening to this conversation. A nasty spoiled little wretch he was, my dear, the only child on the ship, indulged in every way, and always butting into other people's affairs.

"They eat humans, Trolls do!" he squeaked out. "Suck them dry, like oranges!"

"That is so," agreed Yurg, giving little Ollie an ironic nod.

"But what about the lost island?" Herbert persisted.

"Ach, well, mostly it is not to be seen. Only when the Trolls choose. Only one group in sixty or seventy will come across it."

"Because of fog, most likely," said Herbert. "There's always some rational explanation for these folktales. Can one land on the island? It must be a great bird sanctuary."

"One can land when it is there, certainly," bowed Yurg. "Otherwise, instead, we visit a famous cave with bats, where you can go in the boat."

"Bats? Thank you *very* much," I said. "I'll sit that one out."

If there is one thing I cannot abide, it is bats.

The first twenty-four hours, we never disembarked at all; just went on chugging, on and on, endlessly up the fjord. Didn't see much other water traffic. Very occasionally there'd be a fellow fishing; or a ferry, with a few

15

people in it, crossing from side to side, from one dismal little settlement of wooden houses to another on the opposite shore.

"How people can live here!" I said to Herbert. "And why bother to cross? It's the same on both banks."

"I suppose people were born here," he said. "And are used to it. Must be pretty quiet in the winter."

"Winter?" I said. "It's winter now!"

"Nonsense, my dear. Only October."

It certainly was quiet. As if everything were settling down for its winter sleep. Just sometimes the crawk of a bird. Herbert, of course, was wild about *them*. Anything with wings he saw, out would come the field glasses.

He got very riled with little Ollie.

"Mr. Wilcox, Mr. Wilcox!" the boy kept screeching. "Look this way, *quick*! A huge bird with a red breast!"

And, of course, every single time Herbert got there, no bird to be seen.

"It had a red breast and a white tuft on its head," Ollie would tell Herbert. "And it was as big as a chicken—bigger!"

"The sort of bird best eaten with a pinch of salt," *I* said.

For little Ollie, as well as being truly obnoxious, was a born liar. The tales he told of life in Shrewsbury! To hear him, you'd think his parents were like royalty in the town. The only true bit appeared to be that he was a chorister in the Abbey choir. His mother did confirm that.

"He's got a lovely voice," she said, rather sadly. "The pity of it is, he's under strict orders from his choirmaster not to sing *at all*, outside of services and choir practices."

16

So we had to take little Ollie's voice on trust. And were happy to do so.

On account of my disability, I didn't want to move around the ship much. Mostly, after breakfast I'd establish myself in the lounge bar, which had comfortable banquettes—I'll say that for the *Queen of the Fjord*—I'd fix myself up snugly with my sewing, and stay put there till lunch, while Herbert took pictures of the birds. After a bit, people got not to notice me much. I was part of the fittings. And, my dear! the gossip I picked up! That Yurg was having a fling with *both* the girls—Anni and Christa— that the captain was under notice, because he'd got drunk on the previous trip and lost the anchor; that the water supply was liable to run out soon and we'd have to spend a day at one of the fjord-side villages, refilling; that there was no radiophone on board, the only way to get in touch with the cruise management, in an emergency, would be to stop and phone from a call box on shore.

"And there are such a *lot* of those!" I said sarcastically to Herbert, who shrugged. He was quite enjoying himself, in his way.

Meanwhile we chugged on *our* way. Every now and then we'd stop at some small, solitary anchorage, a pier built from huge chunks of granite, sticking out into the black, seemingly bottomless water. And there would be launches waiting, or a couple of coaches, ready to carry us inland, first up a hideous steep climb, zigzagging across the mountainside, then over miles and miles of desolate country, to feast our eyes on something the cruise organizers considered a prime treat—a tiny wooden church, whose main claim to fame was that it had been built four hundred years ago and nobody had bothered to add to it or pull it down; or a waterfall, or a seventh-century tomb; or a glacier.

"Glaciers are only frozen rivers," I said to Herbert. "Why—just tell me why—would anybody want to travel three hours in a coach to look at one?"

With my disability, sitting in a coach for as long as that is no joke, my dear, I can tell you. Though at least the coaches were well heated—more than one could say of the ship—and Yurg did turn out to be quite a good guide, full of tales and jokes and odd bits of information.

He always, on all these trips, wore a medallion on a leather string round his neck. The medallion was made of leather too.

"Was given me by my fiancée, Helga," he told me. "She is a glove maker in the big city. All the time she is making beautiful, beautiful expensive gloves for the fashion houses. Very well-paid work! This medal she makes me for luck, for safety, for insurance, since I must travel so much. She makes me a St. Christopher medal out of bits left over from the gloves. She is a very loving girl, my fiancée."

Doesn't stop you from carrying on with Anni and Christa, I thought.

"Why should a leather medal bring you luck?" Herbert asked.

"Glove leather: it is thought to be very strong luck. Any piece left over from a glove—that is certain to bring good fortune. And protection."

"But why?" Herbert persisted.

Yurg did not know. "It is just so," he said vaguely.

Here another passenger spoke up: Miss O'Mara, a history teacher from Dublin. She was a little silent, weedy spinster lady, who had never said anything, up to now.

"A glove is a sign of good faith," she said, blushing. "It is a very ancient token."

And she went on to give us a bushel of unwanted information about glove marriages, glove money, and glove contracts.

I pointed out to Yurg—who was looking bored, though he was nodding politely—that the leather string which held his medal was coming unstitched. I offered to mend it for him, so he took it off and gave it to me. I put it by for later, as my sewing kit was down in the cabin.

Well, after lunch—yet more fish—we tied up at one of those forlorn anchorages. Two coaches were waiting to take those who chose on another scenic journey to see a ship's grave. A *ship's grave*, I ask you! And yet another waterfall. Anni and Christa were in charge of the coaches. Yurg was going to escort a boatload on a trip up the fjord to look at some ancient rock carvings, runic inscriptions and a picture of the goddess Freyja blowing her horn.

To my surprise, Herbert said he didn't want to go on any of these outings. As a rule, he's quite keen on a boat trip. But it was because—he told me later—little Ollie and his parents had opted for the boat, and Herbert couldn't stand the prospect of being stuck at close quarters with little Ollie for several hours.

"I'll just stay on the bank and fish," he said.

Well, of course, put Herbert by a lake or a pond with a rod in his hand, he'll be happy for days. So I said no more.

A CREEPY COMPANY

Mind, *I* wasn't too wild, speaking personally, about looking at runes and the goddess Freyja, but the boat trip, I thought, would make a change.

Off we went, leaving Herbert, quite contented, on the jetty. When he's fishing, he smokes his pipe. Other times I won't allow it, certainly never indoors. Well, dear, it's a disgusting habit, isn't it.

Turned out there weren't many candidates for the boat. Perhaps little Ollie had put others off as well as Herbert. But also there was a nasty, snuffly cold going the rounds of the ship; quite a few of our group chose to stay on board.

"All the more room in the boat!" says Yurg cheerfully, helping me over the gunwale. With my disability, getting in and out of boats can be a problem; but I had my rubber-tipped stick. And Ollie's father, Professor Kendrick, turned out to be quite gallant, and was a big help too. Between them, he and Yurg guided me to a comfortable seat in the roofed-in section of the launch.

We waved goodbye to Herbert and chugged off up the fjord, under those beetling cliffs. Professor Kendrick was telling little Ollie about the Viking ships, with birds' or dragons' heads carved on their stem-posts, setting out from these shores to ravage the coasts of southern lands. Little Ollie looked bored.

"Not surprising, is it, really, that the Vikings should want to go off exploring to warmer parts," I said to Mrs. Kendrick. "You can see they'd want to get away from their homeland. The mystery is why they ever came back."

It was foggy weather, cold and gloomy and quiet. Slop,

slop, went the water against the cliffs, as the boat's wake fanned out behind us. The sun hardly ever shone here, except when it was due east, at sunrise. Why would anyone take the trouble to carve runic messages on these rocks? You'd think they'd find somewhere more cheerful.

Drifts of fog shifted about. Far up above us a few gulls wheeled, at the top of the cliffs. Here, the rock rose up on either side, steep as a wall. But after a while we rounded a bend of the fjord and saw that it widened out quite a lot; there were rocky islets scattered over a kind of inland sea, which was surrounded by snowy mountains. Nobody— not a single boat—within sight. I shivered, and was glad I'd thought to bring my second-best fur, the one with the thermal lining. On the boat, though, the engine kept us warm.

Ollie said to me impudently, "At least *one* of your legs won't feel the cold."

I gave him such a look!

"Hold your tongue, Ollie," said his mother, but without any real grit in her tone.

She was shivering too.

Now we came to one of the little islands which had a cliff dropping sheer to the black water; Yurg sidled the boat up alongside and we saw the carving of the goddess Freyja riding sidesaddle on her brindled cat and blowing her horn; she was waving her hand, looked quite jolly and carefree. Below her was carved a kind of triple leaf, intertwined.

Yurg made some male chauvinist joke about her.

"You had better not have said that," remarked Professor Kendrick, studying the inscription alongside, the runic writing, which to me looked like a lot of triple Es, and some Rs and Ks made with three strokes.

"Oh, and why not?" says Yurg, laughing.

"Freyja does not tolerate impertinence," says Kendrick. "She was a touchy goddess. When a giant was after her, he'd stolen Thor's hammer, and he offered to give it back in exchange for Freyja; the gods had a serious discussion about handing her over to this giant; Thrym, his name was; and Freyja became so furious that her neck swelled up and scattered her gold necklace all over the ground. The inscription here says:

> *Cattle die, all beasts with cloven   And beasts with pads*
> *hoofs*
> *All must die in the end, but the   Who has insulted Freyja*
> *death of a man*
> *Is terrible beyond belief.*

"Hey, Yurg, doesn't that scare you?" squeaks little Ollie. But Mrs. Kendrick told him to shut up.

Then we went on to another island, where there was a carving of the god Thor fishing from a canoe for a serpent. At least that's what Professor Kendrick said it was. You had to take Thor and the serpent on trust. The canoe was clear enough. I felt sorry that Herbert wasn't with us. He would have liked Thor's fishing rod.

Then, suddenly, Yurg let out a bellow.

"What's up, you run out of fuel?" says Kendrick nervously.

"No, no, but we are in luck, such luck! For there is the

lost island, it is visible today! There it lies, straight ahead, now the fog has cleared."

Yurg's hand is shaking so much with excitement that you'd think it was the Taj Mahal or the Pillars of Hercules he was pointing at, instead of an ordinary, dingy little island. To me it looked exactly like all the rest, just a pile of rock, with a few spindly trees and some reedy grass growing near the shore.

"Can we land on it, can we?" clamors little Ollie.

"If you wish," says Yurg.

So he edges the boat up alongside a kind of rough rock platform and ties it to a metal ring-bolt that somebody has, at some time, hammered into the stone.

"There is a cave on the island," says Yurg. "With another inscription. We go see."

"Count me out," I say. "You know how I feel about caves. I'll just stay here, nice and peaceful, and keep an eye on the boat."

Yurg looked a bit doubtful at that.

"Is best we all stay together," he said. But I was firm. You have to be, sometimes, with those people. They may mean well, but they get above themselves. I had no intention of being pinched, in the cave, by Yurg.

So they went ashore, Yurg, Miss O'Mara, and the Kendricks.

I stayed in the boat, perfectly comfortable, and I won't deny that I seized the chance of a little shut-eye. When they go ashore, other people always take an amazingly long time over what they are doing.

I was woken by a sound.

23

A CREEPY COMPANY

What kind of sound? Lots of people asked that, but, my dear, it's hard to say.

It was like no other sound I've ever heard. A kind of a *stunning* sound.

As if there had been an earthquake, perhaps. And, in fact, some boulders did come rattling and thundering down the rocky slopes of the island. One hit the boat and made it rock.

Now what have those fools been up to, I wondered.

At that moment I saw them come running: Miss O'Mara, and the Kendrick couple, and little Ollie.

White and horrified-looking.

They flung themselves into the boat, and Kendrick cast off. Then he started the engine.

"Hey! Wait a minute!" I pointed out. "Where's Yurg? What about *him*? You can't go off and leave Yurg behind."

"Oh, be quiet, woman," says Kendrick—quite rudely. "Yurg can't come. We have to go and get help."

And he heads away from the island at top speed. It looks to me as if he's more concerned with getting away than with getting help.

"What happened?" I ask again.

Ollie was crying and shaking, his mother white as a ghost, while Miss O'Mara had hunched herself up and was rocking to and fro over her crossed arms as if she had the pain to end all pains.

"The cave fell in," snaps Kendrick flatly. "Fell in on Yurg."

"Cyril, you know that's not true, that's not what happened," wailed his wife.

"What did happen?" I said again.

Miss O'Mara sobbed out: "Yurg set fire to himself with the candle. Oh, it was horrible! And then the rock fell in—"

"With the candle? How could he possibly do that?"

Little Ollie leaned over the gunwale and vomited. His mother promptly did likewise.

"Watch that wretched child!" I snapped—I can tell you, my dear, I was becoming very fed up with them all, and their idiotic stories. And *all* we needed, at this moment, was to have young Ollie topple into the fjord and someone be obliged to go after him. It certainly would not be me. I grabbed him by the scruff, held on to him till he had finished throwing up, and then shook him, none too gently.

"Come on, now, let's have a straight story. What happened?"

Little Ollie looked me in the eye and said, gulping, "It was a Troll. It was covered in blue scales, it had three heads and six arms. Blue flame came out of its mouths. It picked up Yurg and pulled his head off. It was coming toward us, but—"

"But what? What happened?"

"I sang," said Ollie. "Trolls hate noise. I sang a *Gloria* that we've been practicing in the choir. And the Troll turned round and went back, far back into the cave where it had come from. And then the roof started to fall, so we ran out. The Troll took Yurg's head with it."

"That, of course, is total rubbish," said Professor Kendrick, who had a white ring all round his mouth. He gave a furious look at his son. "I'll speak to *you* back on the ship," he said.

"Oh, be quiet, Cyril," said his wife.

"I think I'm going to faint," said Miss O'Mara.

Luckily I remembered that I still had some instant coffee in my flask. There was just enough for a small drink all round. After that, nobody said anything at all until we got back to the ship. Kendrick went straight off to the captain's office. The others made for their cabins, and I looked for Herbert.

He, my dear, was as pleased as punch, because he had caught two sea trout and arranged to have them served for our evening meal.

After twenty minutes Kendrick came out of the captain's office looking irate. The captain sent for Miss O'Mara. Then for Mrs. Kendrick. Then for me.

"Can *you* give me any account of this business, Mrs. Wilcox?" he asked me.

"Not having left the boat, I can't," I said. "Only what the others told me. All their stories disagreed. Professor Kendrick's is the most likely to be true. There certainly was a rock fall. I heard a loud noise, and some boulders fell. Are you going to send a party to look for Yurg?"

"I can't, in the dark," he said.

Of course dark falls early in those parts. It was dusk by the time we got back to the ship.

"Besides, we'll need a professional rescue team with helicopters," said the captain. "I have to telephone for that."

He went ashore to do so, from a kind of coastguard post at the anchorage.

That night the atmosphere on the *Queen of the Fjord* was like a funeral barge. Anni and Christa were both in hysterics. *I* thought about Helga, the girl who had made Yurg his medallion.

Herbert, who had never much liked Yurg, was the only cheerful passenger, because of his two trout. Several times during supper I was obliged to speak to him sharply, and once I had to kick him on the ankle.

Next morning the captain went ashore to phone again, and came back looking pale and startled.

He told Herbert—who told me—that the body of Yurg had been picked up, *ten miles away*, inland. At a place called Skenlønd, or something like that. Yurg was dead. And—this is the part that even Herbert found hard to swallow—his body was completely hollow, empty, deflated, like an orange that has been very thoroughly sucked. The head was separate.

The *Queen of the Fjord* turned round and steamed back to the port where we had embarked. Nobody mentioned Yurg. I still had his medallion, of course. The best thing to do seemed to be to drop it over the side, so that is what I did.

Only one person alluded to the episode. And that was little Ollie. He said to me, as Herbert and Professor Kendrick were helping me up the steps onto the plane that would take us to England: "Anyway, the Troll wouldn't have wanted *you*. Trolls don't eat people with wooden legs."

Toomie

When you travel with a ghost, your problems can be really acute.

Julia and I had hoped, of course, to get off to France without Toomie. But our hope was not even founded upon sand; it was founded on thin air.

As soon as plans for the summer holidays at Ste. Baume leaked out, the demands began.

"Can we bring Toomie with us? Please—oh *please!*"

"We *can't* leave poor Toomie back at home. All on his own! That would be wicked!"

"She'd be so lonely!"

For a long time, it had been thought that Toomie was a boy.

"He wears boys' clothes," said Marianne.

"But that's because it's safer. He's really a girl. He told me so *himself,*" argued Tom, who was two years younger.

"Why was it safer?"

"Because—because—people might hurt him," said Marianne. "His father used to beat and bang him *dreadfully.*"

"But his own father must have known whether Toomie was a boy or a girl?"

"It wasn't really his father—it was only his—his—stepfather."

Large areas of Toomie's life remained pretty vague. Julia and I felt this was just as well, for it had plainly been a short and unhappy one. Nor were we able to discover precisely when he had lived.

Tom said: "He's still alive *now*."

"No, silly, that's only his ghost," said Marianne. She frowned in thought. "When Toomie was here it was a very long time ago. In the war."

She could not tell which war.

"When there wasn't much food."

That might have been any war.

"We've told her about France. We've told him how lovely it is at Ste. Baume. He really, really wants to come."

"She's never been in any other country but England."

Privately, Julia and I hoped that, when it came to the point, Toomie would be unable to leave Camberwell. Surely ghosts don't usually go abroad? But the drive to the airport showed that, so far, the migration presented no problem.

"You can sit between us, Toomie. But you can sit up on top of Tom's pack, so you'll be able to see out. Look, look at all the buses."

And, at the end of the flight, the lady who had shared their three-seat row in the plane said to Julia nervously, "It's really wonderful what imagination children have nowadays, isn't it? I suppose they learn to play these games at school?" before making off hastily into the airport with her hand luggage.

At the Lyons airport our trouble started.

Toomie, it seemed, was fascinated by the luggage carousel. As is always the way, our five large duffel bags were the very last to be extracted from the plane's hold, and in the meantime we had spent half an hour watching other people's wooden boxes, rolled-up mattresses, easels, outsize pink teddy bears, infrared grills, and plaster peacocks whirling round and round on the conveyor belt, unclaimed, and apparently unrequired by their owners. The things that people take with them on their travels! But few of them, I thought, as unwelcome or as inconvenient as Toomie, who, according to Tom and Marianne, now hopped onto the belt, between the pink nylon ted and the infrared grill, and was borne off through the flapping rubber fringe.

"Oh, TOOMIE! Come back!"

"What's the matter, Marianne?"

"Toomie's gone off with the luggage!"

"Don't worry, he'll come back in the other way," said Tom robustly. "Yes, look, there he comes. Oh Dad—can *I* do that too? Can I get on the luggage belt?"

"No, you certainly may not."

"But Toomie did."

"Toomie's a ghost. We aren't responsible for what he does. But you'd better tell him to get off. Any minute now our luggage will come through, and then we're leaving. Yes, look, there is one of the bags."

By the time all our bags had turned up, Toomie, it seemed, had fortunately had enough of riding the carousel and was prepared to accompany us to the car rental counter, where a great many forms had to be filled in. The children grew restless and impatient.

"Toomie doesn't like it here."

"Well, he'll have to put up with it, like the rest of us," Julia said shortly. "Do you want to go to the bathroom? Down those stairs."

Toomie, it seemed, was immune to such needs. One advantage of being a ghost. But when the children came back, they fell into panic and anguish.

"Where's Toomie?"

"I don't know," said Julia crossly. "Isn't she here?"

"No."

"No!"

"Toomie! TOOMIE! *Where are you?*"

At this moment the rental formalities were completed.

"Come on," I said. "Our car is in the car park, at the very farthest end. As usual. Everybody please carry one piece of luggage."

"We've got to wait for Toomie!"

"We certainly have not. If that ghost chooses to wander off, that's entirely his own concern. We have a four-hour drive ahead of us, I'm not waiting any longer or we shan't get there before dark. Come on!"

With Tom in tears and Marianne biting her lip, we humped our bags and struggled across the car park. Even Julia seemed concerned.

"Look—" she said. "I know it's all just—But if we start the trip in such—I mean, it's going to be hard to—Well, I don't know exactly how we—"

Luckily, as we were ramming the last of our enormous

31

bags into the tiny luggage compartment of the hired car, the problem solved itself.

"Oh, TOOMIE!"

"Where *were* you all this time?"

"We thought we'd *lost* you!"

"Will you please tell that ghost not to wander off anymore," I snapped, as Julia stuffed the children into the back with drinks, cookies, comics, books, and listening apparatus.

"He thought he saw Chap," Tom explained, as we threaded our way out of the airport complex and took the road south. "He hasn't seen Chap since he died. Chap, I mean. He's always looking for Chap."

"And who, pray, is Chap?"

There was a moment's silence while explanations were imparted.

"Chap was Toomie's dog. But he was killed. It was very sad."

"Something perfectly dreadful happened to Chap."

"What kind of dog was he?" Julia hurriedly asked, hoping to bypass any account of Chap's dreadful end.

"One of those dogs with flat, squashed-up faces."

"A bulldog? A Boston terrier?"

These terms, apparently, meant nothing to Toomie.

"He was brown."

"And quite big."

"Anyway," said Julia, "if Toomie is a ghost, and Chap is a ghost too, why can't they—well—get together?"

A long silence followed this reasonable-sounding question. At last Marianne said, "Toomie says it's not as simple as that."

"Nothing is ever simple," I sighed. "Look, Julia, can you just tell me which way I go at this hideous junction that's coming up ahead?"

She studied the map.

"You want to take the road to Annonay."

"There isn't one."

"St. Etienne, then. Get quickly into the outside lane."

"Oh."

Luckily, after an hour or so, the children, tired from our early start, fell asleep.

Whether Toomie slept or not, we could not tell. He/she never talked to us.

The hills grew steeper, the villages smaller and more scattered, the roads narrower.

At last, when we were within a mile of our destination, the children woke, yawning, stiff and thirsty.

"Are we nearly there? Oh, good!"

The last mile to Mas Honorat is all downhill. Down a single-track, narrow, precipitous, zigzag track, a dirt road which in winter becomes more of a challenge than any bobsled course. The view is spectacular, but passengers in cars are seldom looking at it; they are watching the distance from the wheels to the edge of the track, or praying, or keeping their eyes on their laps.

Not Toomie, though.

"Toomie says he's never, *ever*, seen anything like *this*!"

"Well, that's nice," I said, feeling for the first time a faint warmth toward Toomie. Poor little south London brat, these French mountains must indeed be a surprise for him. Perhaps he/she had never been to the cinema.

33

Perhaps he/she had lived before moving pictures were invented? Or photographs?

"Toomie says, what a good thing we brought the skateboard."

"You did *what*?"

I had been aware, in a vague way, at home, that Tom, who is one of the chief skateboard stars in his playground, had said sometimes, "Toomie loves to ride with me. They didn't have skateboards when she was alive. She thinks skateboards are really plummy."

If we had a language expert with us, I thought, we might be able to date Toomie's life in London from the use of that word plummy.

"Listen," I said, "I didn't know you were planning to bring the skateboard, and if I had known, I would certainly have forbidden it. Mas Honorat is no place for skateboards."

"But why, Daddy?"

"Look at the gradient."

Some of the zigzags were so sharp that I had to back the car down the next leg, as there was not sufficient room to make a proper turn.

"This track was made for mules, not cars or skateboards. If you went off at the corner, you'd end up at the bottom, in the *fleuve*, probably with a broken neck. No skateboarding."

In fact, one of the first things I did when we arrived at the Mas was to remove the skateboard from among Tom's T-shirts and perch it high, out of reach, on a beam in the unfinished area which would one day be the extra guest room. Mas Honorat had been constructed from the ruins of two farmhouses on different levels of the steep hillside, and it was far from complete. Half of each holiday we spent there was devoted to construction work.

While I was carting beams and mixing mortar and rolling rocks, Julia attended to the garden, which consisted of rockeries and tiny terraces, where grew such hardy plants as could survive deep snow in winter, roasting sun in summer, and the attentions of wandering deer and wild boar. Twice a day we took the children swimming in the river—which meant a five-mile detour down the valley and back the other side, in order to reach a spot that was exactly below Mas Honorat, only a few hundred meters down the prickly mountainside, but, from our side, inaccessible until we could afford to quarry ourselves a track down.

Toomie, it seemed, did not swim. Could not swim. Had never entered water in his/her life (even to wash? we wondered) and had no intention of starting at this stage.

After each of our swimming excursions the children were always a bit subdued for a while; it seemed that Toomie went into a sulk at being excluded from a pleasure we were all sharing.

"Though it is his own fault," Marianne said fairly. "I'm sure she could learn. It's silly of her to get so grumpy."

Back at the Mas, the children and their companion occupied themselves quite peacefully for long spells of time, while Julia gardened and I carried on my building operations. On previous visits Tom had helped, or hindered me, mixing cement and trundling wheelbarrow-loads to and fro, while Marianne played quite a useful part in Julia's garden activities. But this year they kept strictly to their own affairs.

"Well, I suppose it's quite healthy in a way," Julia said, one evening on the terrace, as we drank wine and rested our aching backs, while the children, already in their hammocks, sleepily conversed or listened to the local radio station.

"I wonder if Toomie is picking up any French?" I said. "And what exactly do you mean by *healthy*? Is it really healthy to play with a ghost? I do worry about what he may tell them."

"Well, we've always said it was a pity there aren't any local children for them to play with. So I suppose in a way it's as well they have Toomie."

Ste. Baume could hardly be described as a village. It was a community of scattered farms dispersed over many miles of breakneck slopes. Our nearest neighbor, Madame Berthezène, was within a hunting horn's distance as sound carried or the raven flew, but we were not ravens, and it took half an hour to reach her by car. She was an elderly widow in her late eighties, whose children, and even grandchildren, had long since predeceased her.

"Let's go and call on Madame tomorrow," Julia said. "I've masses of pictures for her."

Madame collected pictures of the English royal family, and we spent our winters chopping them out of newspapers and magazines. The Queen Mother was her special favorite. *"Ah, quel courage! Quelle bonté!"*

When we said we were going to call on Madame, the children, who usually adored her company, were unexpectedly reluctant.

"You'll only talk boring grown-up talk and drink horrible aniseedy drinks for hours and hours. Can't we stay at home?"

"Well—all right; if you'll be sensible."

For several days past they had been absorbed in a slightly incomprehensible game involving the use of a number of sawn-off rounds of tree trunk, fuel for the stove, which they used as stools, or stepping-stones, or building material. *"Don't* move that, please, it's Toomie's palace wall!"

"Oh, sorry. Must he have his palace right in front of the kitchen door?"

"It's the only flat place."

Well, that was true. But, otherwise, it seemed a harmless occupation.

Only once had I been obliged to issue a veto, when they began rolling the rounds of wood down the mountainside.

"Please stop that, it's dangerous."

"Why?"

"Well, firstly, there's a bit of cliff below the house, you can't see who might be down at the bottom. People come there to fish. And no one wants a ten-pound log falling on his head. And, secondly, it took a lot of trouble carting these logs here. We don't want them wasted."

Tom took this prohibition in good part.

"Actually," he said, "it was Toomie's idea."

Toomie, apparently, went into another of her sulks.

"Toomie and Tom like playing boys' games," Marianne later confided gloomily to Julia. "It's not much fun for me with them anymore. I'd rather help you with the garden."

37

"Well, when we come back from Madame's, you and I can plant a row of lettuce seedlings. She says she's got some to give me."

"Can I come with you?" said Marianne unexpectedly. "To Madame? I'd like to see her."

"And leave Tom on his own? No, I don't think that would be such a good plan."

"He'd have Toomie."

"A ghost isn't really enough company," said Julia.

In the car, on the way to Madame's house, she said, "And I'm beginning to think that Toomie isn't a good influence. I'm a bit anxious about what she tells them."

"*I've* thought that all along."

"I wish we could think of some way of getting rid of him."

"Me too," I said with feeling.

"But I don't suppose there's any chance of its happening in France. Perhaps when we get back to Camberwell . . ."

Madame was desolated not to see *les petites anges.* "I have been baking some special cakes for them. Well, you must take them when you go. But please, please bring Tom and Marianne to visit me very soon. Onyx is sad not to see them, also."

Onyx was her immense, blunt-faced brown mountain dog, reputed to have rescued several snowbound travelers in the course of his long life.

We spent a pleasant hour with Madame, who was a kindly, massive lady, exuding bounty. But then she grew unexpectedly fidgety.

"No, I don't like it too much that you leave those children on their own. It is better you should return to them."

In fact we had been feeling the same way, and left her terrace readily enough. Mas Honorat was not visible from her ridge of the mountain.

"As a matter of fact, Madame, they aren't entirely alone," Julia explained, to give the conversation a more cheerful turn, for Madame's brow was furrowed with worry. "They have their ghost friend with them."

"*Hein? Un revenant?*"

Explanations about Toomie took quite a little while, during which I was dying to get away. To my surprise, Madame received Julia's account with total seriousness.

"For myself, I have a complete belief in phantoms," she said. "I am a sensitive, you see, *un médium*, how do you say it in English?"

"A medium. Same word."

"After people die, sometimes it happens that the spirit lingers for a while, confused, lonely, uncomprehending. Then it longs for company. So that is why, doubtless, this sad little ghost has attached itself to your pair. But it is not a desirable relationship."

"No, *that* it isn't," I agreed. "But why do you think so, Madame?"

"Because it will be most natural that this ghostly *copain* may wish that one of the children, or both, should also become a spirit. So as to ensure permanent companionship. Whereas, of course, this Toomie should be working to free himself from all the ties that still attach him to this world and his former life. And traveling on to greater freedom."

"Yes, I see. And I quite agree."

"I wish you will go home *now*, at once," said Madame forcefully.

I drove as fast as I could; but you really cannot hurry on those tracks.

At the top of the drive down to Mas Honorat we met Marianne, looking tearful and distressed. She hurled herself into the car.

"I was coming to get you! Toomie has talked Tom into getting down the skateboard."

"But how could he possibly? How could they reach it?"

The ladder, I had taken care, hung high enough so that Tom, on his own, could not get it down.

"Oh, they are piling up those bits of log to make a staircase. And then they are going to ride down The Slope. *Please* hurry, Daddy."

She was on Julia's lap, and I was featherstitching my way down the zigzag with infinite, frantic, desperate care.

The Slope was what we called the forty-five-degree angle of mountainside that connected all the zigs and zags of the track. A long, lethal slant of it lay above and on the far side of the house. I did not dare look in that direction, as I guided the car down onto its usual stopping place, but Julia suddenly said, "I can see them," in a voice so dry and faint that it sounded as if her throat was full of sand.

I leapt out of the car and shouted, "*Tom!* Stop that!"

"*Tom!*" screamed Marianne. "Toomie wants to *hurt* you!"

Julia had raced into the house. I could not think what for, until I saw her reappear, dragging the enormous beanbag which served us as a sofa on wet days.

"You brilliant woman!" I croaked, in a voice as dry as hers, and helped her shove and haul it up the dusty slope, and place it in the track of the oncoming Tom.

"*Wheeee!*" he was shouting. "Isn't this *plummy*! Hey, Toomie! We must be going a hundred miles an hour!"

The beanbag stopped them. Stopped Tom and the skateboard, at all events.

Tom was considerably cut and grazed. But what really shook him was our passion, and our rage against Toomie.

"He didn't mean any harm. *Honestly*, Daddy. It was just a game."

"You are not to play with Toomie *any*more. At all. *Ever*. And I am going to chop up the skateboard and burn it."

Tom went weeping off to his hammock.

The atmosphere at Mas Honorat was dreadful.

"Toomie's terribly upset," Marianne told us. "And angry, too. He doesn't understand at all why you are so cross. And, actually, I don't see how you *can* stop Tom playing with her."

Nor did we.

"I'm going to go and see Madame," said Julia.

While she was gone, I carried out my threat, chopping the skateboard into firewood, removing its wheels, and stuffing it into the stove. While I performed these actions I felt surrounded by cold, malignant silence. It took no effort at all to imagine Toomie at my elbow, watching, speechless, furious, waiting his chance to do me a bad turn.

When Julia returned, Madame followed behind in her own car.

"In our hurry we forgot Madame's delicious cakes,"

Julia said, and took them into the children's room. A silence lingered behind her as she emerged; I hoped very much that it came from contented nibbling.

Madame sat upright in our wooden armchair. Onyx, who had accompanied her, placed himself with gravity, equally upright, beside her.

"Tell me again what happened," said Madame, and listened, nodding, to our account.

"It may well be, as Tom says, that the little *revenant* meant no *harm*, in our sense of the word, to Tom," she then pronounced. "After all, to him, death is no different from life . . . *Eh, mon Dieu! Regardez Onyx!*"

The monumental and dignified Onyx was lying on his back, waving paws in the air, an expression of idiotic bliss on his face.

"Toomie is rubbing his stomach," explained Marianne, who had come quietly from the children's room. And she added, in a low voice, "I believe Toomie thinks that Onyx is Chap."

"And who was Chap?" inquired Madame.

"Chap was Toomie's dog."

Madame nodded. "Who knows, maybe it was so? Who knows if dogs have souls too, and can come back? Maybe those two arranged, long ago, to meet here?"

She addressed the air.

"Toomie? *Ecoute, mon enfant!* You are now coming home to live with me, and Onyx. *Comprends-tu?*"

"Can you *see* Toomie, Madame?" whispered Marianne, awestruck.

"Almost," said Madame Berthezène, with her severe smile.

I knew what she meant. I myself had *almost* seen Toomie sitting on Tom's shoulders, atop of the skateboard.

Madame got up and left, Onyx following. We heard the sound of her car starting and driving off.

Marianne went into the children's room and said, "Tom: Toomie has gone to live with Madame and Onyx."

A very long silence followed. Then Tom muttered, in a choked, tearful voice, "Well, perhaps it's a good thing. Madame always said she was sorry not to have children in her house. And we can always go and see Toomie when we come to stay here."

I suppose that is true, I thought, with little enthusiasm.

But a cold, early autumn set in that year, after we had left Ste. Baume at the end of August, and a ferocious, freezing winter. Blizzards and avalanches were frequent. One of the avalanches swept down the mountainside and removed Madame's house, with her inside it, Onyx, her furniture, and all her pictures of the British royal family.

"Perhaps she and Toomie and Onyx are all keeping each other company somewhere," Tom said sadly, when we received this news.

But I hoped that Madame, and Toomie also, had traveled on to a greater freedom. As she herself would have put it.

The Thing-in-Waiting

Mind you, I blame what they call the Media. All them newspapers, TV and radio programs, *Who's New*, *Up Your Way*, local interviews and gossipy chat shows and feature stories with a smitch of this and a touch of that. Weren't there all that rubbish blown and poked and dribbled into folk's ears, nobody betwixt here and Land's End would ever have heard of our part of the country, nor about Orris Place, nor Lady Elfrida's Christmas lily. We'd ha' stayed quiet and comfortable, not thought of, nor visited, like we been for the last nine hunderd years.

But there you go. Once a person—or a place—turns into News, they don't rightly belong to theirselves any longer. And that's bad. That can be terrible sad.

Orris Place weren't all that big. Nor it weren't writ up in a lot of guide books, because it were main okkard to get to, even the quickest way to Orris lies all along of our little twisty roads through the marshes, roads that seem to career right, left, and rat's ramble, and can take you miles out of your journey, given you don't know which exact turn to take at every little crossroads. The signs all tell different stories. Place names come and go as if the sign-makers just meant to befoozle strangers. There's a rhyme said in our parts:

> Criss-cross east
> Five at least
> Criss-cross west
> Half the rest
> Only one
> Leads straight on
> And that will wind
> Out of mind
> Afore your journey's done.

Pretty fair jabber, it be. Unless you know where to start from. Or where you aim for.

It's said there was allus a big gentry house on the site at Orris Place, since long before Roman times. And the history folk, them as know, could point you the various bits that were left from one bygone time or another. Part of it was big old square blocks of stone, that's from the Romans, they allus left their mark tidy and workmanlike. Then there was a part standing on legs, that was put up by Saxons, who chose to keep the cattle underneath and sleep warm and dry up above. Then the Normans dug a moat and put up a chapel and builded a tower. Main fond of towers, they Normans. Then King Henry Eight, he added on a wing, and Good Queen Bess, she clapped on another, and Queen Anne, she stuck on a fourth side. So it ended up as a square, with a cobbled courtyard in the middle, and the moat running round outside.

A real mishmash, you might say, a bit of this and a bit of that. But not big. No, the whole place not much more than a tidy sizable farmhouse with a tower at one corner. And a little old pantry-size chapel next the tower.

Along the side of the chapel a row of heads. Inside the chapel, the tomb of Sir Alured Hamley, who died at the Fall of Antioch, in one o' they Crusades. His widow traveled out next year and brought back his corpus, and afore that she voyaged on to Jerusalem and out beyond, so 'tis told. 'Twas from that journey that she brought back the lily, along with her husband's bones.

She was a learned lady, so the tale goes, knew a deal about herbs and medicines, could talk to you in Latin and Greek and they Eastern lingoes. It's said she did a power of good to the folk in the fens and marshes, a fair-dealing landlord, gave money and food for a plenty charities. One story has it that, when she was out in the Holy Land, she went to visit the Old Man of the Mountains, Hasan i Sabh, or Rashid ad Din—some say one, some say t'other—so as to hold learned conversation with him. And while she was there she was able to cure the favorite one of his hundred sons, who was lying mortal sick of a fever. In return for her saving the lad's life, the Old Man gave Lady Elfrida this lily bulb. And he told her that it would go on living and flowering for a thousand years, so long as one of her family was still alive to tend it, in the place where it was planted.

Well, be that how't may, there allus *has* been some of

the Hamley family at Orris. And the lily's allus bloomed, regular as sun-up, at Christmastide. Not on Christmas Day, but at the first stroke of midnight on Christmas Eve.

Seen it? Oh yes, I seen it, plenty times. Just a tiddy small flower, it were, not one of your big, gaudy, show-off blooms, but a thin stem with flowers up it, about the size of a lily-of-the-valley. The color was enough to burn your eyes—a deep, deep ruby red. And the scent! It crept on you like smoke, and put a kind of wonder into your mind, enough to make you remember things that never did happen. And then 'twas gone, in a flash.

You could travel half the world over, and never find another like it.

How come I seen it? My Dad and I would mostly be at Orris around Christmastide, staying in the Queen Bess wing, where there was allus rooms for workers on the estate. Stone-cleaners, we are, see. Leastways my Dad passed away, nine years come St. David's Day, but I still keep up the old trade. There's not so many of us left, now. Travel round the shire, we do, from one big house to another, a-scrubbing of the stonework and statuary, a-scraping off the moss and lichen, repairing, repointing, making all newlike and vitty. There's many a big old mansion fine and square-standing this day, that would ha' been all scrumbled away, or covered up in moss and ivy, 'tweren't for me and my Dad and others like us. Stone is like skin, it needs care; only lasts a few centuries longer than skin, 'less you look after it. 'Tis a good life, faring about the shire, sleeping a week or two here, a week or two there. Suits me. I like to think while I work. Night-times, in some cool, ancient stone-walled sleeping-loft, I like to read. Read what? Why, the Scriptures, o' course. There's enough in they books to last a man his natural life.

Anyhow, that's how I first come to see the Orris lily, on a fine frosty Christmas, dunnamany years back, when Dad was still in his prime, and I was a hopeful young 'prentice, my rheumaticks didn't chaw on me like they do now. (That be the dread bane of our trade: it do come from keeping still, hours together, in some okkard spot, perched up a ladder all stiff and twisted and stretched, no way to move, scrubbing and scrubbing away at some old stone gargoyle. That's the way all your bones and sinews get pulled out of true, clenched amiss, and 'tis mortal hard, after days and weeks passed so, to unclench 'em again.)

So, as I say, this Christmas feast found us at Orris. The frost had held for weeks, all the marshes, mud and reeds, was friz over. So was the moat round the big house, clear marble-green ice right down to the mud bed at the bottom. And the thorn trees likewise. All beyond the moat and across the marshes there's a multitude o' those, blackthorn, buckthorn, hawthorn, every kind o' thorn. And in this winterlong frost they was all furred over wi' white, and shone in the sun like filigree.

I spoke of the row of heads along the side of the chapel. Sir Alured was the first, and his wife Lady Elfrida alongside of him. And the rest was more family. Sir Alured's grandson got to be a baron, and *his* grandson got to be an earl. But they kept the name, never changed it. Then the title died out, for the earl's son was killed in some battle, and he had only a daughter, but she married a cousin, so there was still Hamleys in the house. The heads was put up later, sixteen hunderd or so. They took the likeness of Sir Alured offn his tomb, and that of Lady Elfrida from the portrait at Waldey Abbey. (She gave money to the monks there to have masses said for Sir Alured's soul, as he died in battle, no time to be shriven.)

The minute I saw Lady Elfrida's face, I thought, You're the lady for me. And I cleaned her up main careful, with my sponges and cleaning fluid (that was a secret 'twixt Dad and me. Every man in the trade has his own secret).

'Twas a handsome, strong face, with flowing hair under a little circlet, and deepset eyes. Mouth half smiling but firm. Looks like she'd take no aggrification from anybody. That was the best part of my work. I felt a kind of closeness between her and me, as if I recognized her. And she recognized me, too. "I'm your man, missus," I told her.

After that, every Christmas when I come back—"How's it been, then, this year, Lady Elfrida?" I'd ask her, in my mind, like; and she'd look back, calm and friendly, and answer me in her own way. She cared for her folk, were they grand or simple, if they belonged to the place.

Down below, alongside the chapel, under the row of watching heads, that's where the lily grew. (Course the heads weren't there when she planted the lily, they was put up later.)

There was a little stone-walled 'closure, about the size of a chicken-run. Very snug and sheltered, 'twas, caught the sun all day, and screened from our north and east winds, which do come cutting and whistling here, straight from that old north pole. That was the corner where Lady Elfrida set the bulb the Old Man of the Mountain had given her. Likely she had the wall built round it, special. And that's where the lily stayed for the next nine hunderd years, or as near as be bothered. (Fine black rich soil we have hereabouts.) 'Tis told that Lady Elfrida used to feed the plant with dried blood; oxblood that'd be, mostly, for it was all oxwagons here in those days. Anyhows, the plant throve, and spread, and prospered. But grow in any other spot it would *not*. If a bulb was broke off and planted elsewhere, if one was given to a friend or neighbor, it would always pine and dwindle away.

Queen Bess when she came to stay here, with the Hamley of that day (Earl Maurice, I bleeve), you may reckon that she was fair wild to have a bulb, and they gave her one, of course, you can't say no to your liege Queen, but 'twas no manner of use. She took it away with her, and fed it on dust of gold and pearls, likely, but it died.

My first Christmas at Orris Mrs. Hamley came to me and my Dad, as we was a-cleaning up the rows of saints around the chapel doorway, and she says: "You'll dine with us in the Hall tonight, Mr. Wragby, and your son too, of course?" We said we'd be proud to.

That was what was allus done, at the Hall; Christmas Eve, all the folk that worked on the estate, cowmen, smiths, ploughmen, woodmen, shepherds, masons, were all bidden to the big Hall (that was in Henry Eight's wing) for Christmas Eve dinner. Like a Harvest Festival dinner, 'twas, only with Christmas puddens and pies. Mrs. Hamley, the Mrs. Hamley of our day, was one o' the family too, and had married her cousin. She was a short, stocky lady, not the way I think of Lady Elfrida. But she had a straight eye and a keen look to her, upright, old-fashioned; and a friendly word for all there, knew their children, down to the last newborn. And her husband, that was also her cousin, Mr. Gervas Hamley, he were an affable, handsome old gentleman too, but ailing with a murmureous heart. Had to be wheeled in a basket-chair.

After the dinner, and after we'd sung "For they are jolly good fellows" and a tidy few Christmas carols besides, all the people moved out into the courtyard. There we stood waiting, quiet and regardful, along by the Queen Anne wing, that my Dad and I had just been cleaning.

I noticed Mrs. Hamley look at her watch and then at the chapel clock, anxious-like. (The yard was all lit up with lanterns and flaring torches.)

She said something to her husband, and he shook his head.

"They're a-worrying about young Mr. Edward," Mr. McGregor the head gardener told my Dad. " 'Tisn't the first time he's cut it fine."

Mr. Edward was the son, supposed to be studying science and medicine at Cambridge College, but, by all accounts, he was a wild young spark and spent more time than he ought up in London, playing cards in gambling clubs with some havey-cavey friends, when he should 'a been studying his books.

But anyway, when the hand of the chapel clock was creeping on toward midnight, we begin to hear the sound of a motor, way off, across the marshes, and—wonderful fast, considering 'tis a bitter old night, and the winding roads all slippy with ice—that motor comes roaring over the moat-bridge and in under the arch, where no trades-man is ever allowed to drive. And what a motor we see—a big, long-snouted open-top racing job, wheels like pump-kins, and all its tubes on the outside, that made enough roar for the Day of Judgment. No doors to it, Young Mr. Lordly just steps over the side, in his gloves and goggles.

"Did you think I wouldn't make it, Mother dear?" he says, laughing, careless-like, and Mrs. Hamley she says, "No, no, of course, dearest boy, we knew we could rely on you," and old Mr. Hamley in the wheelchair, he coughs and gasps out a Christmas greeting to the lad. But his face was drawn and gloomy, and I thought as I looked at him, You poor old gaffer, you're not long for this world. And maybe glad to leave it.

For Mr. McGregor had told my Dad that already Mr. Edward's debts and doings were a heavy weight and trou-ble on the old man.

Well, we all move in around the little old stone-walled penfold where the lily grows. During the daytime 'twas covered with a big half-transparent waterproof sheet, to guard it from the weather and any dust that might blow about from Dad and me cleaning the stone round about.

I've allus been a tall gangly one. Which is right useful in our trade, for I've a long reach, and, with my brushes and cleaning sponges, can get to corners that a shorter chap could never stretch to.

So—besides not wishing to seem pushful—I'd stayed at the back of the crowd, sure enough that I could see over folk's shoulders, when it came time for the lily to bloom.

And I saw two things.

The crowd of estate people had left a space, a pathway, between two groups, so that Mr. Hamley in his wheelchair, and his wife and son, could move straight to the low wall, only knee-high in front, that was round the lily-pen. And now, as it come to midnight, they moved slowly along that path.

Mr. Edward pushed the wheelchair, and I happened to glance sideways at his face, when he was a-passing me. And the look on that face turned my blood almost as cold as the marble-green ice in the moat. For it was black with discontent, with grudge, and sour-mindedness, and boredom. I could see that, for two ha'pence, he'd yell out with annoyance and spite, that it drove him wild to be obliged to come back home, year after year, and take his part in this ancient fuddy-duddy practice, which, plainly, he saw as something left over from the Stone Age, something only suitable for kids, and yokels, and doddering old nincompoops.

I wondered how long he would go on putting up with it, if that was how he felt. But perhaps he was obliged to?

Then I looked back past Mr. Edward, across the middle of the courtyard. And there I saw a mighty queer thing.

There's that story in the Scriptures, that I like to read, every while or so. About Lot's wife. How she looked back at the doomed city and got changed to a pillar of salt. From the very first time I read that tale, I had a clear notion of what a pillar of salt would look like. And in the middle of the Orris courtyard, now, I saw what looked to me like the ghost of a pillar of salt. A bit taller than me, 'twas, and no special shape to it, just tall and thin; taller and thinner than a tall thin man would be, if you take my meaning; and, furthermore, I could see clean through it, to the stonework and moldings on the Queen Anne wing that my Dad and I had cleaned that morning.

There it stood. Or hovered.

Now I heard a long drawn-out breath, an "Oooooh!" of wonder, and turned to see that, as the chapel clock clanged out the first stroke of midnight, so Lady Elfrida's lily had bloomed. And the crowd begins to move forward, slow and civil, each pair giving way to the next, for a short, fond study of the bloom. Nobody outstayed their turn, but you could see that each pair, after they looked, was sad to trudge off and give up their place. Dad and I took our turn, and smelt that wonderful scent, delicate and spicy both, that seemed to blow from beyond the other side of the globe.

Then we shuffle onward, and, not long after, are both in our beds in Queen Bess's wing.

"Dad," I said, "did you notice a kind of a *thing* in the middle of the courtyard, time the lily bloomed?"

"Kind of a thing, what kind of a thing?"

"A kind of a misty column—like, say, the ghost of a statue."

But no, he hadn't.

"Get off to sleep now, boy," he grumbled. "Too much Christmas ale! Your mind be full of moonshine."

Next day I chanced to be at a job of cleaning on the portico of the old garden temple, alongside of Mr. McGregor, who was working on a hedge nearby. So I mentioned the matter to him. (—No, I'm telling a lie, not next day, which was Christmas, and a holiday, but the day after. Those times, folk took no account of Boxing Day.)

"Mr. McGregor, is there any tale about a kind of a

thing that might be see'd in the courtyard, time that lily blooms?"

Mr. McGregor gave me a slant look, over his pruning hook.

"You saw it, did you? It's not all that can. I can myself— being Highland born—and Mrs. Hamley can—but there's a deal of folks wouldn't know what the pize you were talking about."

"What is it, Mr. McGregor?"

"The family call it the Waiter," he said. "So Mrs. Hamley, she told me."

"The Waiter?" I thought of a chap with a tray, and a napkin over his arm.

"Summat that's waiting," said Mr. McGregor. "I reckon it's been waiting ever since Lady Elfrida first brought back the lily. Come to these parts *along* of the lily; to guard it, you might say. To watch over it."

That made sense. There had been such a powerful feeling about that shape: watchful, unflagging, biding its time.

"Some of they big grand plant nurseries," Mr. McGregor said, "that sell foreign species, young trees, plants that's real rare and precious, they won't let one o' their stock go without there's someone at the other end that's qualified to care for 'em. And if there's nobody, why then they send out a qualified person, till the tree, or whatever it be, is well bedded and settled in."

Well, that made a kind of sense, too. But, *for nigh on a thousand years*? The Old Man of the Mountain, I thought, must have had a great regard for his lily.

After that, I allus used to take a look in the lily pen, going and coming. Once the red flower was gone by—it only bloomed for a few hours—there was little to see: just a mess of spiky leaves. Lady Elfrida's stone face looking down from above.

Now and agen, come we was at Orris over Christmastide, I'd see, in the middle of the yard, what, in my mind, I'd come to call the Thing-in-Waiting. It never budged from its place, and few but me ever seemed to notice it. Just sometimes I'd notice a body give a queer, puzzled glance as, maybe, they brushed clean through the silent, patient shape, or past it. Myself I'd never do that. I kept a decent distance, like you would from a sign that says: Danger, High Voltage.

Well, times went on, and times got worse. Poor old Mr. Hamley, by and by, he took and died, and the Orris estate got run down; land was sold off, workers were laid off. Mrs. Hamley came sadly to Dad and me at Christmas and said, "Mr. Wragby, I'm feered I can't afford to ask you to come anymore, after this year."

"Ma'am, I'd do the work for nowt," he says, very shocked; but that she won't have.

She looked thin and pale, all shrunk away, like a little owd withered leaf. I'd never ha' thought that a stout, well-fleshed lady, as she did use to be, could wane and shrivel so, in a few years.

"There's bitter trouble atwixt her and young Mr. Edward, now he's got a position up in London City," Mr. McGregor told Dad and me. "He's got this smart young-lady friend now, Miss Vondra del Mayo. One o' they journalist females."

"Yes, I heered of her, I bleeve," Dad says. "Seen her on television."

"Very like. She's on TV more than she's in her own bed, by all they say. And she writes for various o' they shiny magazines, *Yours* and *Hers* and *Ours*; special for one called *Patrimony* or *Symposium* or some such, all about furniture and pictures and fashions in summerhouses."

Mr. McGregor picked a snail off the bush he was pruning and dropped it in a pail of salt water. I reckon he'd have liked to do the same with Miss Vondra del Mayo.

"What she and Mr. Edward want is to have Orris Place open to the public. He says that'd make a sight of money, pay off all the debts; and *she* says 'tis a shame that such a grand old place 'is not available to the man in the street.'"

"The man in the street'd never find his way here," I said. "He'd end up down on the seashore."

"But what about Mrs. Hamley?" Dad asked. "What does she say?"

"She's set against any such notion. She says owd Mr. Hamley'd turn in his grave. And, what's worse, Miss Vondra del Mayo is keen to have one o' they TV programs come and film the lily when it flowers. 'So,' she says, 'the whole world can share in this wonderful epiphany.'"

Fine words, young lady, I thought. But maybe there's some things as the whole world is not meant to share. Some things is supposed to be kept small, to each group of folk for their own.

"What does Mrs. Hamley say to *that*?"

"She can't abear it. I heard her shout out, 'Over my dead body!'—they was in the Yew Tree Walk, and Mr. Edward getting right nasty about it. 'You do realize, Mother, you are turning your back on thousands of pounds?' he says, cold and drawly. Seems that's the fee they offer. 'And I've had dozens and dozens of requests from newspapers and magazines. News of the lily is getting about.' 'Turn my back?' Mrs. Hamley cries out. 'I wish I could turn my back on you two forever. I'll not allow it! And that's my last word. You know what it says in your Father's will.'

"Seems, in Mr. Hamley's will, he left orders forbidding any such thing, unless his widow was to give permission. And it's plain she never will. But just the same," Mr. McGregor went on, "stories are starting to be printed in magazines about the Orris Place lily. 'England's Secret Treasure,' they call it. I reckon Miss Vondra del Mayo is at the bottom of it all."

So, times went on, and times got worse. My dear old Dad died. Then I read in the paper that Mrs. Hamley, poor lady, she had a stroke. Not long after that, I read in another paper about her funeral at Orristhorne All Saints, and how she was to be laid to rest in the chapel at Orris Place, alongside Mr. Hamley.

Humph, I thought. Now's your chance, young Master Edward.

And, sure enough, he took it.

The house was thrown open to the public. Next thing, there's new signposts all across the marshes, with a little drawing of a mansion-house inside of a lily flower, and a hand pointing, and "Orris Place" lettered up big in fancy lettering.

I didn't go there to see. I'd no fancy to see all the world and his missus paying their three-pound fee, and then a-peering and a-gawking at those things I used to take such care of, Lady Elfrida's head and Sir Alured's tomb.

But, come next Christmastime, I got an invite.

"We are reviving the fine old custom of inviting all those connected with the Orris Place estate to come and be present at the flowering of Lady Elfrida's Lily, which will also be shown on North Sea Television," said the printed card. "Drinks and a buffet supper will be served in the Henry VIII Hall from 10:30 on Christmas Eve. Admission £30.00."

Well, I ask you!

Pride would ha' kept me away, anyhow, but, as mischance 'ud have it, I'd lately given my back a nasty jar, a-falling off a ladder at Frisby Castle, and so was stuck abed.

I telephoned Mr. McGregor (these days he was working for the Duke of Colchester) to ask if he'd be at Orris Place, but he said no, wild horses wouldn't drag him. " 'Tis a wicked shame what's happening at Orris," he said. "Mr. Edward got married, last autumn, to Miss Vondra, and now they plan to open a theme park, and a waxwork show, and a bingo hall, and an ice rink. They reckon all that will be funded by the fee they receive for the TV viewing of the Christmas lily."

Come Christmastide, flat on my back though I was, half shamed at my own inquisitiveness, yet I could not keep from switching on the program. I was wishful to get a last view of Lady Elfrida. And that I did.

First they showed a distant view of Orris Place and its moat. That must ha' been taken weeks before in autumn-time, red berries on the thorn trees. For now 'twas bitter cold again, iron-hard frost all over the marshes.

Then we saw the thorn trees, guarding the place like prickly ramparts.

I thought of the Ancient Britons, and the Romans, and Saxons, all the folk after them, who had lived in that place and called it home.

Then we had a shot of King Henry's banqueting hall, and the guests all guzzling down their thirty-pound Christmas dinner.

"It looks warm and festive in here," the commentator told us. "But outside the temperature is bitter cold, ten degrees below freezing. Even the River Fleme is solid in its bed."

Then we saw the customers gathering in the courtyard. Not quiet and reverent, as in Mrs. Hamley's day, but all bustling and excited, little kids, mums and dads, young couples laughing and joking, happy to be asked what they had to say, and none of them *did* have much to say, beyond what a big thrill this was, and such a different Christmas from last year, when they were at Auntie Sharon's.

Then we saw young Mr. Edward and his lady. She'd been a brunette, but she'd turned auburn since I last saw her on TV.

He was saying: "Of course I myself have been present at this ceremony ever since I was a small child."

Yes, I thought, and how sour and bored you were. How you wished you could get the blazes away from it all.

"Now," he went on, "we are so glad to share it with all these friends. And, in, future, we hope to share it with

many, many more; for the lily is to be taken and propa-
gated by an expert from the National Arboreal Institute of
the U.S.A. We are going to divide the bulb and so permit
many, many other friends to enjoy this unique experience.
The main bulb will be in California, where it will be
tended most carefully by Mr. Courney Hansell Window,
the great American orchid expert. We are sad to lose it,
naturally, but Mr. Window will soon be sending us back
offshoots from the parent bulb; and what he gives us for it
will be sufficient to put the Orris Place estate back on its
feet again. Mr. Window will tend the bulb just as well as
the Hamley family have done here." He glanced up at the
clock and finished quickly, "So here we say goodbye to
the Orris lily for a few years. But we are sure that it will
thrive in its new home."

The camera moved up to the row of heads above him. I
saw Lady Elfrida looking down. Goodbye, my dear Lady,
I said to her, inside my own mind.

I had heard a few gasps from the crowd, as they took in
what Mr. Edward was saying. And my own breath seemed
to have stopped.

Now the camera moved down again, focusing, close-up,
on the lily, and we saw its tiny, blazing-red petals begin to
spread, as the clock tolled out its first stroke.

And then, suddenly, there was a flash, and a lot of confusion. The screen went blank.

"Excuse me," said the lady back in the studio, "we seem
to have lost the picture. I'll transfer to another camera."
And then she cried out in amazement: "Good heavens!
One of the stone heads has fallen right on our camera!"

The picture came back, but it was pitching about, people were running and shouting and screaming. Another of the heads could be seen falling—Sir Alured this time.

"I'm afraid Mrs. Hamley has been hurt," gulped the lady commentator. "Oh, my goodness!"

Now the picture showed us all the big yard at Orris, the crowd lurching in confusion. But, in the middle of it all, I could see the Shape, white and misty, calm and motionless.

Then it began to move, silent as a cloud passing along. Straight across the space it steadily went. Young Mr. Edward turned, and I could see that he saw it advancing toward him. I could not hear the scream he gave—the sound was lost—but I saw his mouth open wide. Then he was whirled up in the Shape and carried clean through the chapel wall, and out of view.

Then the lady said, "I am so sorry, there seems to have been some kind of interruption to the Lily Festival at Orris Place, we are returning to the studio."

Next day I read in the paper about how they only just got the guests out of Orris Place before the whole building went up in flames. No one knew what could have caused this, the insurance company was fair mystified, for the fire seemed to have started everywhere at the same single moment—chapel, tower, east, west, south wings all blazed up like a barrel of tar and sawdust. Not one stick left to stand on another. The stonework all reduced to black, powdery dust, Lady Elfrida as well as the rest.

And the lily? Not a shred left, not a leaf, nor a petal.

But here's a queer thing.

Mrs. Hamley—Vondra del Mayo that was—she'd got

killed by Lady Elfrida's head falling on her. And Mr. Edward, *he* was found, bedded *deep* down in the frozen moat. Nobody could understand—then or after—how he could have got underneath all that ice, solid marble-green to the bottom.

However he'd got there, dead as a mackerel, he was.

But away across the marshes from that spot, they found a *path*. As if something—something wonderfully hot and fiery—had passed along through the frosty thorn trees, a-melting and a-withering. And the grass was all browned and burned, like as if a hot fire engine had passed that way. All across the frozen marshes, so far as the coast, that straight, burned path took its way. And, on the sandy sea-shore, it was lost.

Which way did it go? Why, eastward. Back to the Old Man of the Mountain, I reckon.

They Have Found Out

Mr. Caspy was having a good time buying a ball-point pen in Woolworth's. A clipboard with paper attached lay chained to the counter, and Mr. Caspy tried quite a number of pens before fixing on the one that seemed best; it did not do to take one that yielded up its ink too freely, or it would run out too soon. He liked to get good value out of his pens, and became extremely annoyed if one of them ran dry under its allotted span of two to three years of use. He always wrapped a tiny jam-pot label, with the date, around the pen as soon as he got home, so that he might know what to expect. And if it expired prematurely he took it back with a complaint. In the same way he marked his marmalade, whiskey, apple juice, and milk, so that due measure could be kept on consumption, no commodity used up too fast, or too slowly. (That anything should be consumed too slowly was, of course, not at all a frequent occurrence.) In the same manner margarine, cheese, and bread were marked by faint knife lines, indicating the day's, or the meal's, portion. Mr. Caspy had grown up in World War II, when almost every commodity was rationed; the methodical and orderly habits thus engendered in him had never been relinquished.

Having finally selected his pen, Mr. Caspy carefully surveyed Woolworth's, a haven to which he paid regular visits, calculating that the cost of the bus ride was well balanced by the savings on articles bought there. He enjoyed, as well, the dazzling light, the warmth, all free, the slightly gritty feel of the narrow-planked floor underfoot—as if glass powder had been sprinkled over it—the perfumed air, redolent with bath essences and inexpensive makeup, the bright colors, the shine and spangle of tin and tinsel, and the confidence engendered by the fact that every article on sale had its price clearly displayed. There was never any need to ask, and be betrayed, by embarrassment, into an unnecessary purchase. Mr. Caspy hated asking the price and had more than once forgone some desired object rather than make an inquiry about it. He had a nervous dislike of admitting to ignorance, which had often stood him in bad stead.

Now, having come to the conclusion that nothing else in the shop was, at that juncture, necessary to him, he carefully tore off the strip of paper on which he had tried out the ballpoints, rolled it, and tucked it into his jacket pocket. Why make a present of his handwriting to some stranger?

Turning into Smith's, the stationers, he bought adhesive tape, string, and a small telephone note pad, all of which he knew to be on sale cheaper here than in

Woolworth's. (The Woolworth's pad, at first sight, *appeared* to be a better bargain, but in fact had fewer pages; the tape and string were both longer at Smith's.)

Then, satisfied, he caught his homebound bus, proffering a return-half ticket which had, of course, been bought at half-price on his Senior Citizen card.

There was a calm pleasure in the slow progress of the bus; while many passengers fidgeted or tapped their feet impatiently at red lights and blocked traffic in congested streets, and then at slow meanderings in the open country and along little-used roads in order to take in the maximum number of rural stops, Mr. Caspy merely thought complacently what a lot of mileage he was getting for his money, and how very much his ride would have cost had he been so reckless as to take a taxi. In fact as the bus jolted along he fell asleep, and had a brief but vivid dream: he was seated on a hard bench in the Tuileries Gardens, and was observing a sparrow, with something in its beak, which was being energetically pursued by a gang of other sparrows. It zoomed across the space in front of him, at last dropping its treasure, which proved to be no more than a used yellow Metro ticket. Emily, beside him on the seat, did not think this as funny as he did. She was saying, "Can't we go and have some lunch, dear? I'm awfully hungry—and, after all, we *are* in Paris—it does seem a shame—" and he was saying, "No, no, you'll appreciate your dinner all the more if you work up a good appetite for it."

Mr. Caspy woke up as the bus jolted to yet another halt, glanced at his watch, and was pleasantly surprised. His time was insufficiently occupied on the best of days; this inching progress would most handily dispose of the bald, empty space between two and four, quite the worst part of the day. At four it would be permissible to put on a kettle and make tea, saving the tea bag for future use; at five some acquaintance might telephone, and Mr. Caspy could also go out to feel his washed socks on the spindle in the back garden to see if they were dry; at six there was BBC news, most respectably occupying thirty minutes; and, after that, the careful, meticulous preparation of a frugal evening meal permitted another hour, at least, to slip by; then the meal could be slowly consumed, washed down by a medicinal glass of whiskey on doctor's orders; then television or radio, eked out by the remains of the morning's newspaper, supplied a satisfactory bridge leading from supper to his solitary bedtime. Mornings were much better. They had an impetus of their own, supplied by the daily harvest of mail, mostly, these days, bills, catalogs and bank statements, but still, something had to be done about them, they could not be allowed to lie dustily or mount up; there was also the newspaper and the need to purchase food and household articles.

It was life; it passed.

Whiskey, thought Mr. Caspy, in annoyance; he should have bought a bottle at the big cut-price store next to Woolworth's; how could he have forgotten? There remained in his current bottle only enough for another eight and a half days.

He took out the new ballpoint and made a memorandum in the tiny notebook he carried always in his jacket pocket. Out, at the same time, came the tiny rolled slip of paper on which he had tried the pens; with a touch of bewilderment he read his own writing:

"They have found out and are coming to get you."

What nonsensical impulse had sent those words into his head? What was their origin? Where could he have read, or heard them? On television? *Who* have found out? Found out *what*?

Flushing with exasperation, stuffing the tiny roll of paper back into his pocket, Mr. Caspy glanced at the last page of his notebook and was reminded that, after leaving the bus and before going back to his house, he had an appointment at the local doctor's office to receive the result of a routine checkup.

One should make the most possible use of the National Health Service, Mr. Caspy believed; after all, it's our money that pays those scroungers.

Minutes later he was sitting on the hard velvet bench, staring out with impatience at the little fountain that played to itself in the clinic courtyard. What do they need *that* for? he grumbled to himself. It was a total waste of electric current, all coming out of the taxpayer's pocket, mere ridiculous decoration and titivation. However, disciplining himself to ignore the frivolous play of water, Mr. Caspy picked up a leaflet on the subject of *Cystitis and You;* after all, one ought to benefit from the free literature they left lavishly lying around.

A bell rang, and he jumped uncontrollably; really they ought to adopt some more civilized, some more dignified, means of summoning patients to the doctors' offices. Patients were not slaves, after all!

"I'm afraid it's not good news, Ted," said Dr. Owens. "Though not, perhaps, entirely unexpected?"

Mr. Caspy stared, as if, to him, the news was not only unexpected, but wholly, outrageously incredible, invented as a piece of monstrous tomfoolery, some demonic practical joke . . . Meanwhile, the doctor went on talking.

"How long is it since Emily died? Fifteen years? Well—" the doctor spread his hands, as if to indicate, we none of us live forever, do we, and you are a good age after all.

"But *she* died of anemia—nothing to do with heart—" objected Mr. Caspy in a tone full of resentment. He stood up, and gave the doctor's cell-like office a sour scrutiny, as if in search of some appliance which he could not see there.

"Well," said the doctor again, "think over the choices I have given you, and we'll discuss them again in a few days. I don't think—"

What the doctor did not think, Mr. Caspy did not wait to hear. He had already turned, angrily snatching up his plastic bag with the string, adhesive tape and telephone pad—string! A whole large new ball of green, glistening string, guaranteed good for outdoor as well as indoor use! And a memo pad at least half an inch thick! Two hundred pages . . .

Proceeding more slowly than was his habit along the quarter-mile walk from the clinic to his cottage, Mr. Caspy observed three temporary road signs—red-bordered white triangles, set up along the grass verge to alert motorists:

A CREEPY COMPANY

They make motorists slow down for toads, thought Mr. Caspy morosely, but not for pedestrians, oh no. At present there were no indications of toads; perhaps they preferred to perform their crossing at night. Where were they traveling *to*? Why did toads wish to get to the other side of the road? What happened to them there?

Did they ever go back?

Arrived at his own gate, Mr. Caspy saw with annoyance that some person had been through the gate and had left the metal hasp thrown back, not hooked over the gatepost. The postman probably, stupid, careless, indifferent fellow. If a wind had blown up, there was only a frail, ancient latch to hold the heavy wooden gate; it might easily have blown open, slammed and swung all afternoon, knocked the whole gate right off its hinges. And the gravel path needed raking again, gravel was all scuffed to the side, tufts of grass growing in the middle and dead leaves, slippery, dangerous. He must speak to Jim Ward, tell him to rake it. But who for?

Scraping his shoes carefully on the metal grid by the door—one *paid* for the gravel, after all, no sense in carrying it indoors—Mr. Caspy turned his key and entered the dark house.

Of course it was not really dark, only dusk, and he walked into what—since Emily died—he had thought of as his den. It faced west, catching the warm honey-colored light of the setting sun, and was, especially at this time of day, his favorite spot in the house. An old red Turkish carpet, acquired secondhand at a hotel sale, covered the floor; a leather-covered couch and armchair, much worn but comfortable, and a battered rolltop desk, crammed with dusty papers, made the room indisputably his, a male domain; Emily's leather-framed photograph on the desk seemed present on sufferance, like the token female member of a committee, existing to prove lack of prejudice.

With an exclamation of annoyance Mr. Caspy moved to right the photograph, which for some mysterious reason had fallen onto its face. Could there have been a mild earthquake? Or—conceivably—burglars? But no, all else seemed undisturbed.

Then, glancing round him, Mr. Caspy let out a second gasp—of disgust this time. For, all over the dark-red carpet, where oblongs of late sun revealed the worn, dusty condition of the pile, Mr. Caspy now saw the silvery tracks of snails—or slugs—crossing and recrossing the warp. Hundreds and hundreds of them!

Dropping the bag on his untidy desk, he hurried back to the kitchen for the vacuum cleaner, assembled its component parts, plugged it into the socket under the desk (a most inconvenient location), and proceeded to give the carpet a vigorous going-over, muttering, "Horrible—foul—revolting," as he worked. "How could they have got into the house? Where are they now? There must have been a hundred of them," he said again.

The cleaner flashed its red light, indicating that the dustbag needed emptying, and Mr. Caspy almost snarled with annoyance. This was his least favorite of all household tasks, and the evening was drawing in, soon it would be time for the BBC news and his glass of whiskey. But things must be done properly and in order: he switched off the cleaner and pressed the Bakelite catch to release the lid at the end of the barrel-shaped body. The dustbag was certainly full to overflowing with packed, gray, gritty, hairy dust—the very last object ingested being a tiny furry roll of paper.

Mr. Caspy unrolled it and read again the words, *"They have found out and are coming to get you,"* in his own handwriting.

With a snort of impatience, he poked it back into the dustbag and carried the whole thing out to the trash bin behind the back door, where, by the porch light, he began the careful, distasteful task of sorting through every handful of dust before consigning it to the bin. One never knew what might get accidentally sucked up; vacuum cleaners were far too powerful these days, quite unnecessarily so. There! A penny! When he was young no cleaner could have sucked that up. And half a dozen large bits of gravel, which he carefully returned to the path. Gravel costs money. And the top of a pen—that might come in useful. But to whom? Indignantly, as he avoided some shards of broken glass, Mr. Caspy reviewed the contents of his house: the half-rolls of toilet paper in both lavatories, the almost new cakes of soap—the towels—the good pair of new walking boots. The four inches of whiskey.

Turning, with the emptied bag in his gritty hands, he saw, illuminated by the porch light, a procession of toads hopping one by one through the back door.

"Aaaaargh!" screamed Mr. Caspy. "Just *wait* till I get after you!" and he rushed past them to reassemble the vacuum cleaner. "Just *wait* till I get at you!" he shouted again furiously, scrubbing with his jacket sleeve at the beads of sweat that rolled down his brow and cheeks.

Three days later Mr. Caspy was discovered by the indifferent postman, who, finding it odd that the back door had stood open on all his last visits, stepped inside and found the householder lying on top of his vacuum cleaner. It was concluded by the coroner that Mr. Caspy must have given himself a lethal shock in pulling out the plug; considering the state of his heart, the doctor said, quite a mild shock would have been sufficient to carry him off.

No toads were seen. Presumably they had proceeded to their onward destination. But Mr. Caspy had been rather disagreeably nibbled by slugs.

The Ferry

Judith stuck up a sprig of holly and then looked round for another site. She still had an enormous bundle to use up, but there wasn't a single space left indoors, and she gathered up the scratchy, rustling armful and took it into the porch to form a sort of berried nest which would, she hoped, look cozy and encouraging to callers.

That done, she went outside for a moment to gloat over the house. They had been in it only a fortnight and it still seemed hardly credible—to be here, beside the sheet of glimmering water with gulls crying plaintively above, instead of inhabiting the dusty warren of a suburb with Ken catching the eight-thirty every morning. How a not very large legacy can alter your life, she mused; a month ago we thought of Cornwall only as an ultima Thule, a horizon to be attained some time after the age of sixty; and now here we are, already equipped with a boat and some hens, and Ken off getting in the Christmas drinks.

The house was small and white; Judith thought that it looked rather like a shell left lying by the water with firelight throwing a pink glow on the walls inside and the curved steps leading down to the landing-stage. It had been the boatman's house when the ferry was running, and was still called Ferry House. The hill rose up, steep and bare, behind it; there were only three other cottages on this side of the river and they were farther out toward the point. The village proper was all over on the other shore, and she could see lights beginning to shine out from windows down by the water and the colored gleams from the pub Christmas tree on the quay.

It was cold. Judith shivered and told herself that she had better go indoors and begin changing for the Martins' cocktail party. But for some reason she felt a strong reluctance to go indoors and an even stronger impulse to stay here idling on the landing-stage. She would have liked to sit down and dangle her legs over the side as if it were an August afternoon instead of dusk on Christmas Eve. She knew now that decorating the porch had been only an excuse to get outside the house.

"But why?" she demanded in protest of that other Judith who was so dumbly, insistently urging her to stay out on the landing-stage. "You've simply got to get used to being by yourself, you city dweller. There are bound to be lots of times when Ken is out and you can't get into a state of jitters whenever you're alone in the house. It's a nice little house, a dear little house, there's nothing whatever the matter with it."

She stood staring at the black square shape of the open door with the wide water and the lights behind her and felt as if she were at the entrance to a rat hole.

With a strong effort of will she stepped inside. After all,

Ken would be back at any minute with the drinks—she
strained her ears for the chug of the motorboat—and
soon they would be starting off for the Martins' party.
Everything was all right, everything was fine—so why was
she standing in a corner of the kitchen like this, wringing
her hands and biting her lips in an agony of nerves?

Angrily she shook her head and ran up the stairs, took
out her favorite dress, tomato-colored wool, and dragged
it on over her head. Then once again she found herself
standing fixedly, hairbrush in hand, by the window,
straining her eyes to stare at the landing-stage steps. The
telephone rang as she recrossed the room.

"Darling?" said Ken's voice. "Look, a tiresome thing's
happened. The engine conked out on me as I was starting
back. Old Weaver thinks he can fix it in an hour or so in
time for us to come home from the Martins', but it means
I can't get over to fetch you. Can you come over with the
Joneses?"

"I've an idea they went over early to do some shopping.
I'm not sure—I'll go and see."

"Well, call me back if they can't and I'll try and find
someone this side to fetch you. I'm at the pub."

"Right, I'll only be five minutes."

With a feeling of relief and purpose she hung up and
started along the waterside path to the Joneses' house.

"Like it in Ferry House?" asked Mr. Hocking the landlord, hanging red and green paper balls over the bar in
preparation for opening time. "Settling in all right?"

"Yes, we love it," Ken answered. "We're very happy

there. Has the house any history, do you know? Wasn't there a lot of smuggling round here?"

"No, there's only one story I've heard about Ferry House," said Mr. Hocking slowly, "and smuggling doesn't come into it. It happened a long time ago—in the witch-burning days. There was an old woman running the ferry called Mrs. Poysey and it was generally believed in the village that she was a witch. Well, nobody cared much—live and let live is our motto in these parts and always has been—but the squire got to hear the story and he said she ought to be ducked if she was a witch.

"There's a custom round here—used to be, that is, when the ferry was running—that the ferryman took everyone over for nothing on Christmas Eve. In memory of St. Cradock, whoever he was. Of course people used to give a present instead, so it came to the same thing.

"Well, one Christmas Eve the squire, with four or five men, came down to the ferry and asked to be taken across. They'd all been drinking and they carried bundles under their arms saying they were presents for Mother Poysey. She untied the boat and started pulling them across, but halfway over they undid their bundles and took out ropes hung with lead weights, tied her up, and dropped her overboard. Her body was never found. Oddly enough, on the following Christmas Eve the squire himself was missing, and his body was found later, washed up on the White Rocks out by the headland. So people began to say that she appeared in her boat on Christmas Eve offering to take people over on the ferry for nothing, but if they accepted they were never seen again.

"Of course it's a lot of nonsense really—I've never heard of anyone who actually claimed to have seen her. A chap *was* drowned last Christmas and washed up on the White Rocks, but that's where the ebb takes anything floating down. He was a stranger; people said afterward he'd been seen trying to find someone to row him across."

"Jolly," Ken commented.

The telephone rang.

"It's for you," Mr. Hocking said.

"Oh, hullo, darling, is that you?" came Judith's voice. "Listen, a lucky thing's happened—Mrs. Jones *had* gone already, but just as I was walking back I met a funny old crone with a boat who's going across to the village so she's going to take me. Of course I offered to pay her, but she said she'd do it for nothing as it's Christmas. So I'll be over in ten minutes. OK?"

"Hey—wait, *Judith*—" he said frantically, but she had hung up. "Exchange, get me Polhale three-twenty again, please."

"I'm sorry, there is no reply," said the girl after a moment.

Ken ran out onto the quay and stood by the lighted Christmas tree, staring across the water. It was really dark now and the tide was coming in fast, bringing a fog on its back. He could not see the lights on the far shore. There was cold behind the fog, too—he shivered, straining his eyes and ears, wondering if he could hear the creak and splash of a boat or voices in midriver. But there was no sound.

———

When Judith hung up she hurried outside again.

"I won't keep you a moment—I must just powder my nose," she said to the old woman. "Goodness, you do look cold. Won't you come in and have a cup of tea while you wait? I've just made some."

The queer old thing seemed to be shivering uncontrollably. Judith caught at her hand—heavens, it was like ice—and drew her in.

"Do sit by the kitchen fire, it's lovely and warm—I was just wishing I had somebody to share it with. Do you take sugar?"

"I thank you, Ma'am." The crone sat stiff and upright in her rusty black clothes. "I used to live in this house once." But she hardly glanced round; her eyes were fixed on Judith.

"*Did* you?" said Judith, powdering her nose at the sink mirror. "It's a lovely house. You must have been sorry to leave."

"Yes, I was sorry to leave."

"Do have one of my mince pies—they're quite good this year. Oh, you haven't begun your tea yet. Drink it while it's hot, it'll warm you up." She was chattering in her relief at having company at last, and hurried off to get her coat.

Ten minutes later when Ken jumped out of a borrowed boat he saw his front door wide open, casting a square of light down the steps. The house was quite silent.

"Judith!" he called.

The holly in the porch caught at his sleeve as he raced

through. Judith lay in one of the armchairs by the kitchen fire. At his entrance she sat up dazedly and rubbed her eyes.

"Ken! Goodness, how extraordinary—I must have gone to sleep. Where's Mrs. Poysey?"

"*Who?*"

"The old woman who was going to take me across. I suppose she got fed up and went on. She was rather odd—a little crazy, I think. She said, 'You've got a bold heart, my dear. There's few cares to take sup with Mother Poysey,' and something about her house being in good hands at last. I suppose she moved farther up the river when she left here. What are you looking at, Ken?"

He was staring at the other chair. Draped over it and tangled round the untouched cup of tea and mince pie was a mass of sodden rope, to which were attached a number of little lead weights.

"What on earth . . . ," exclaimed Judith.

"Those were what they weighed her down with," he said. "Let's hope she's free of them now."

Little Nym

They comes and they goes. And, mainly, there's fewer of 'em goes than comes. That's on account of little Nym. Furriners from outside don't know about little Nym, and nobody living here in the village is liable to tell about him—why should they? You don't go gabbing to folk from other parts about troubles and shames in your own home. And little Nym's was a black shame.

His trouble would be nigh on a hundred years ago now. My dad—and he died ten year ago come Michaelmas, he'd have reached his hundred next August—Dad's older brother Bert was fourteen when the bad thing happened. Uncle Bert remembered it all, plain as the bombers in World War II. And he told my dad. And Dad told me. And there's plenty others in the village had it handed down in the same way, quiet-like. But it's not spoken about in the street, nor written down in histories.

'Tis on account of little Nym that, time and again, Hawksmoor Hall comes up for sale on the house agent's list; we'll see that old photo they always puts in the paper, showing the big twisted chimneys and the gabling; *Handsome Period Residence*, it says; and weeds begin to sprout in the drive, and Blishen and Pankhurst's FOR SALE board nailed to the gate. Then a new lot will come, and start all over again.

The house ain't bad; if you've a mind for all that oak paneling and polished floors and great big open fireplaces. (I've sheltered accommodation myself, a nice little flat in the Penfold Council Estate, with gas heating and wall-to-wall carpet; that suits me right well.) But, summer and winter, I've been in Hawksmoor Hall, many and many a time, and felt nothing spooky there. Chimney sweep, I used to be; I reckon I knows all the chimneys for twenty mile round like the palm of me hand; a sweeter set of chimneys you won't find than those at Hawksmoor. (Why *Hawksmoor*, don't ask me; there's no hawks and there's no moor; the house sets in the middle of the village, lying back a furlong or so, behind a birch coppice, so's you don't see it from the road.)

When I give up the chimney sweeping I worked for a spell as painter and plasterer with my cousin Fred Muffett the builder, so I been into Hawksmoor plenty times doing work there; and, like I say, felt no harm in the place.

What I did feel was little Nym; and that was in the garden.

Being as the house has changed hands so often, the new folk coming in always wants summat done, or summat altered; new paint in the big downstairs room that faces southerly toward Tarbury Down, or a new bathroom taken off of one of the first-floor bedrooms, or a kids' playroom fixed up in the attics. There's a rare old rats' ramble of attics up there in the Hall; I reckon little Nym musta slept in one o' them.

Nigh on a dozen times I musta been up there in the house working, painting, plastering over a fireplace for one lot of newcomers, or pulling the plaster off again for the next lot. "Just whatever you say, Marm, yes, it do seem a shame to cover up all that there Tudor brickwork." Or, "Yes, the old ranges musta been right okkerd to manage. Nothing like a nice modern Aga to make a kitchen feel cozy."

And all the days and weeks I worked in the house, on my lone or with others, I never saw nothing nor heard nothing. Bar a few creaks in the joists. And you get those in new buildings, just as often as in old. More, if the truth be told.

But after they've put in their new partitions and fancy cookers and built-in bookshelves and double glazing, the new folk never bide long; sometimes they are out before the daffs have bloomed twice in the garden.

Rare lot of daffs, up at the Hall; I reckon they've been a-growing and a-spreading for over a hundred years. Old Mus' Pettigrew had 'em put in, 'tis said, and the snow-drops too, that grow under the big cedar in the middle of the south lawn; regular carpet they are, come February, if it's been a warm winter. *Lord* Pettigrew, he got to be, by the end; raised up to be a lord, on account of all the poetry he wrote, according to what I heard. And had dinner with the old Queen, and all. He had the garden planned out new, and dunnamany trees planted; but then, after the business of little Nym, they moved away and he built hisself a big house on Telegraph Hill; turned that into a museum, the County Council have now, but I never troubled to go there; I got no time for museums.

Turned jobbing gardener, I done, when I come due for me old-age pension and retired from the building trade; that's how I happen to take care of the garden here, two days a week; Blishen and Pankhurst keep me on, even between times, so's the place don't run back too much after folk have moved out.

And that's how I come to have a notion of little Nym.

See him? No, I can't rightly say I done so. But a notion of him, yes, that I do have.

Poor little beggar. He don't mean no harm to me; nor to any soul, rightly, I daresay. Though it do be the young'uns that comes to grief on account of him. Me, he don't take a mite o' notice of; except, once in a while, often of a damp dripply day when the mist lays low over Tarbury Down, the kind of day when there'd be no grown folk about the garden and he could run free; or, when the season's turning, cherry leaves a-reddening, or when the wild hyacinth leaves start to show in the wintry orchard grass; then I'll feel little Nym like a quickness in the air. I'll feel him close by me, or over there, t'other side of the cabbage bed with his head up, sniffing the breeze, keen as a terrier. Mortal full o' questions, he seem to be, at such times: what makes the trees grow? what makes the blue of the sky? why does the earthworms tug down the birk-leaves under the mold? why do the moldwarp travel in a straight line, how can he know to do so if he be blind?

All these things little Nym musta wanted to answer to, once, and not a soul about the place troubled to talk to him or take any notice. I can feel his pain, sharp as a sickness, burning and burning.

Ugly, he were, see, poor little spirit: big head, like a balloon, tiny slanting porker's eyes, and big ears that drew out; besides that, a big red marring birthmark as if summun had turned and given him a swipe; he never growed big but was puny, with arms and legs no thicker than peasticks. And the others: all so big and handsome, the boys, or bright and purty, the gals, never took no notice of him. How do I know that? There's a photo, just one, in the Parish Journal for 1884, showing the May Day Revels: there's the whole family in the garden here, a-watching the crownation of the May Queen. You can see Lord Pettigrew, as he were by then (why they'd turn a chap into a Lord just for writing a whole mess of poems, don't ask; seems a daft-like thing to do); anyway, there he be, thatch o' white hair, white beard long as a hank of hay, tall and skinny; and there's the rest o' the young'uns, eight altogether, the lads in their tight pants and short jackets, the gals in muslins and frilly drawers and sunbonnets; and, peeking out from behind one o' them, this little runt, with an ugly face and a scared look on it, as if he knowed he shouldn't be there, knowed the others are all sick ashamed of him.

He was the death of his mum, see; she died when he come into the world. Maybe, if she'd not, matters mighta turned out otherways.

'Twas the year after that picture was took that they all flitted to Telegraph Hill.

All but little Nym. He'd died by then.

In them times, o' course, they didn't have no Health

A CREEPY COMPANY

Visitors, nor Social Service Workers, nor Probation Officers, nor all the other busybodies that's allowed to come pestering now, knowing your business bettern than their own. Not that it seems to make a heap o' difference, plenty times. Kids get ill done by now just as much, many a beating's handed out, from what you reads in the paper.

Most in gineral it'll be a family that moves into Hawksmoor Hall. "Family house" it's always billed as; the passel of attics, eight bedrooms, tennis court and stabling, who'd think of taking it but folk with a mort o' children? And a regiment of servants? And with Tarbury Down just there across the medder, so all the young'uns has to do is scamper over the stile and off, when they want to get away from Dad and Mum, or the governess and under-nursery-maid.

But little Nym couldn't run. He were lame from birth and could only doddle about.

Anyway, as I said, in the main it's big families that take the house. And, time and again, there's been a death. Time out o' mind. Most times it'll be one of the young'uns. And nearly always the littlest. You'd think word woulda passed around by now, would have got to the new buyers, but no; seems there's always a new lot as hasn't heard, happy to put down their cash for a roomy, handsome brick-and-stone house, with a fine well-planted garden, and stables, and all, so close to the Downs.

They lays down their cash, they buys the house and settles in. Next thing, a kid has died. Sometimes 'tis one cause, sometimes another. Croup carried off little Teddy Laleham; young Marcie Mildenhall took the measles very bad and died o' that, with complications; Annette Blakeney got meningitis and was gone in three days though they whipped her into St. Magnus Hospital over to Portsbourne; Thomas Weller had a fall off his pony and died of a busted neck; little Grace Kellaway, the latest of them but one, she just pined away. That's what *I* called it; her mum had a fancy name for it, Anny-rexy Nervosa.

"Oh, Sam," she says to me with tears in her eyes, "try as I will—try as we *all* will—we *cannot* make her eat enough. Can't you try—if we bring her dinner out of doors? She's main fond of you, Sam—please help us!"

It was true, the little thing used to follow me about when I was a-digging or planting-out; I say little, for she looked about seven, though I believe she was going on twelve. They'd moved to the country hoping 'twould help her; but it only made her much worse.

"Won't you eat your nice meat and taters, Gracie?" I'd say to her, as she'd sit on a pile of bricks nigh me in the greenhouse. "There be ice cream to foller, Mrs. Huckley told me."

"I don't fancy ice cream, Sam," she'd answer, gulping. "And the meat and taters tastes *horrible*—like garbage that's rotted away, like old slimy cabbage. I can't stand it."

Not enough to keep a wren alive, would she take. O' course I knew the reason for it well enough. But, like I said, we don't mention the tale hereabouts.

I done my best though.

"Marm, you gotta get her away from here," I told Mrs. Kellaway. "This house ain't wholesome for childer."

A nice lady she were, but no manner o' use when it come to argufication. "Get her away where 'tis warm, to France or one o' they furrin lands," I told her.

A CREEPY COMPANY

"It's no good, Sam," she'd answer, "my husband don't believe in going abroad. 'We fetched her here, to this beautiful country spot, what could be better than that?' my husband says, and I can't budge him." A nice lady she were, but no gumption to her. So the end of it were that little Grace died—buried in the graveyard here, she be, under the red may tree—and *then* the family shifted off to Somerset, Tiverton way, for 'twas too sad for them here, the memory of her; they'd all been mortal fond of young Grace.

Tell them about little Nym, no, I didn't; anyway, if I had, they'd never have beleft me.

After the Kellaways left, six month went by, but, come May, when the bluebells and pheasant-eyes are out in the orchard, along comes a new lot. Yanks, these ones are; Spooner, the name is, and the chap, Professor Spooner, has hisself a job teaching social science over the Down at Portsbourne University. Then there's his lady and their daughter, little Brooke. That's a funny name to give a girl, I reckon, but Mrs. Spooner told me 'tis an old family name. Different to all the rest, they don't have a big tribe of kids, only the one little maid. "We'd ha liked more," Mrs. Spooner told me, "but it wasn't to be." Friendly, talkative lady, Mrs. Spooner, and powerful keen on old churches; she'd be out and about, all over the county, looking inside of 'em and taking brass rubbings. No, she don't take little Brooke along with her. "Brooke has her hobbies as I have mine," she says. "American children learn to be independent of their parents early on, Mr. Standen." Independent is one thing, thinks I, left alone for hours on end is another; to be sure there was a Danish

88

gal in the house, did the cooking, Uttë they called her. Deuce a bit of time did she ever spare from her house-work and her fancy health magazines to look after the kid. "Is not my job," says she, when I carries in a basket of broccoli. "They hire me as cook, not as nurse." So young Brooke runs wild in the garden and woods, and I worry about her, special when I begin to notice she looks pale, and not as lively as she done when they first come to the place. Coughs a bit, now-and-now.

Ought I tell Miz Spooner about little Nym, tell her the place is death for a kid (and they with only the one), tell her to get the pize outa there afore 'tis too late and they're sorrier than sorry? Days I spend all of a bivver, wondering what's best to do.

Blishen and Pankhurst won't thank me for giving the house a bad name. Like as not, I'll be given my leaf to go. And who's to keep any sort of an eye on young Brooke *then*?

Skinny little 'un she were, not floppy like poor Grace but wiry and windshook; she liked to climb trees, and soon skinned her knees on most o' the big ones in the garden.

First, little Nym didn't trouble her. *I* could feel him, though, a-standing off, watching; in rain or sun, fog or shine, he'd be there; studying and wondering. But then he begun to move in, trying to make her notice him. That were the time I dreaded; when the air round the place begin to buzz, like it do before a storm, when you can feel a heaviness, there's midges a-biting and the birds fly low.

What I said, little Nym didn't mean no *harm*, but he had to make his mark someway, poor young devil, he was main set to make folk mind him. And his own kin, his older brothers and sisters, all so spry and personable, they'd never neighbor-together with him.

Stony-hearted lot, they musta been. To have treated him the way they done, in the end.

"I'm puzzled by Brooke's cough," Miz Spooner she says to me. "Where can she have picked it up? There's no kids in the village—more's the pity—Dr. Venables assures me the air here is very healthy—she's never had such a brontical cough before. I can't understand it."

Dry, short cough it was; shook her poor little thin chest.

"We're going to try letting her sleep in the Garden Room," says Miz Spooner. "Dr. Venables thinks that a good plan; that way she'll get plenty of fresh air."

I didn't think that were such a grand notion, but no-body asked my advice. The garden room had been built on by the Mildenhalls—or the Blakeneys—on the side o' the house facing the shrubberies and Harry Neale's hun-dred-acre field. It was mostly glass, glass walls and glass shutters that would open.

They set up a cot-bed in there for young Brooke. She liked it fine.

"I can hear the birds so loud and the hedgehogs grunt-ing. It's great to have my own door."

There's a glass door, leads straight out onto the lawn. "I can get out real early," says Brooke.

She could get out real late, too. One evening I'd come back after me dinner to do a bit of watering. Bone-dry that May weather were, not a drip of rain fell the livelong month. I'd come back to give my young pea-plants a drenching. Owl light, it were, with a bit of a glim in the sky. You could just see across the grass.

Professor and Mrs. Spooner were away over the Down at one of his college meetings, and the Danish girl indoors somewhere with her eyes pinned to the TV.

I knew I'd have the garden to myself—apart from little Nym, that is. I gets on with my watering and prensly the moon comes up. Print moonlight, 'twere. Then I was fair dumbfoundered to see the Garden Room door open, and young Brooke come a-wandering out dressed in her night-things.

"Now then, Missy," I start in to say, " 'tis time young'uns like you oughta be abed and asleep—" and then, dannel me, I sees that asleep she *be*, though her eyes be open; she don't heed me no more than if I was a rose-bush, but goes mouching along, over the lawn to the cedar tree; I follows her, all in a twit, case she start in to climb the tree, for, thinks I, I'll be obleeged to wake her then, 'tis too dangerous; but I'd allus heard it's best *not* to wake folk that go a sleepwalking, if you can someway coax and gentle 'em back to bed.

"Back to by-land, now, sweetheart," I says, no louder than a huss of wind, and young Brooke she mutters, "Wait—wait—" kind of busyfied and sidy, as if she were on an urgent errand and couldn't be fussed with me just then.

The cedar has big twin trunks and a crack betwixt 'em; young Brooke stuck her skinny arm into this crack, clear up to the shoulder, as if she were a-seeking for a thing she'd laid there and knew just where 'twas; sure enough, she pulled out her fist with summat in it—'bout the size of a crab apple, 'twere; and then, calm as a clock, she turned her round and backwent softly over the grass and into the Garden Room again. I followed along, mortial curious to see what she'd took out of the tree, and found she'd laid her down on the bed again, still fast asleep, still clutching the thing in her bony little fist. Covered in bark-muck, 'twas, and mildew, but I could see it were an old broken mug, lustrous pink in color, with speckles of gold.

My heart did thunder at that, I can tell ye. For well I recollects the story of little Nym.

Quiet as I'd tweak up a groundsel, I slipped it out of her hand, but at that she stirred and cried out, "No! No!" right anxious.

"Don't you fret, sweetheart, 'tis here on the chair," I says, and that calms her down; she goes to sucking her thumb like a two-year-old. So I covers her up and tiptoes away, locking the door behind me, goes round to the kitchen and hands the key to the Danish gal, who's in her own little parlor studying *Glamour* magazine.

"The young'un's been a sleepwalking," I says to her. "Best ye keep an eye on her and be sure to tell the missus."

Uttë just shrugs, as if 'tis no matter to her, takes the key, and goes back to her book.

Next day I comes up purposely to see Miz Spooner, but the gal tells me she and the gentleman are off to London for an educational conference and won't be back till termorrer. That did put me in a frit.

"Leaving none to care for the liddle maid?" says I.

"She gets her meals reg'lar," says the gal, a bit huffy. "I

don't see as you've any call to set yourself in a hoe about her."

I could see I'd get no good out of that one, so I goes looking for young Brooke and found her by my potting shed where there's a water-butt. She'd got the water running from the spile and was rinsing the broken pink mug she'd fetched outa the cedar, doing it as careful and thorough as if 'twas a piece of Crown Derby she'd come by.

"What's that you have there, my love?" says I. And when she answers, my heart fair come into my mouth.

"It ain't mine," she says. "It b'longs to that boy I see standing outside my glass door at nighttime. I'm a-rinsing it for him."

"Boy, what boy?"

Not that I doesn't know full well.

But he never *showed* hisself before.

"He stands at my door and looks in. I seen him a-plenty times," says Brooke.

"We better hang a curtain over that door, then, my deary. It ain't right he should look in your private room."

"Oh, he could see through a curtain, I bleeve," says she. "What's his name, Mr. Standen?"

"His name, deary?" I was all of a pother, didn't know whether to answer or not. "Why, his name's little Nym," I told her in the end. For I reckon she was bound to find out.

That day was the first of June and, like it often happen, the weather turned over. From being bone dry, it went to dank and dripply, misty and moist—the kind of weather little Nym liked best. Maybe his elders, his brothers and sisters that was so hard on him, maybe they didn't fare out o'doors when it was wet; maybe then he had the garden to hisself.

And young Brooke was the same. Try as I would, I couldn't get her to stay indoors, with her storybooks and games, where she'd be safe from him.

"Where we come from in America, it's on the edge of the desert, ye see, the Mohave Desert, Mr. Standen. We don't get foggy weather like this. I think it's beautiful. You can see things that look like ghosts, and the trees are mysterious."

She *would* stay out in the garden, all the day long, and sometimes I'd hear her coughing, and sometimes talking to herself.

Or was she talking to little Nym?

Come darkfall, when the Danish girl called her in to bed, I bethought myself 'twould be best if I come up and slept there, in the garden. There's a middling small summerhouse, what Miz Spooner calls a Grotto, along at the far end of the grass plot, facing out to Tarbury Down. I made me up a bed with two-three old hop-sacks and layed me down there. 'Twasn't too handy, for it faced away from the garden, so I couldn't see what befell there, besides it being a black clungy night. But I slept light enough, waking every half hour or so; then I'd doddle out to look in at the Garden Room glass door, and make sure was the liddle 'un sleeping as she ought. And the first five or six times I looked in, there she lay, quiet as a pitcher of flint.

Then—I dunno how come, I reckon I musta been fair

rasped out with worriting—I buzzled off into a deep slumber. And what woke me next was lights and voices all across the garden, and folk rowsting about every which way, and a lot o' turmoil and tarrification.

Forth I went—'twas still dark as the inside of a cow—and found Professor Spooner and his lady and two-three other folks, all a-hunting and a-searching, with lanterns and torches, all of 'em calling high and low: "Brooke! Brooke! Where are you? My honey, where are you? Come to us, darling—come to us, Brooke!"

Then Miz Spooner catches sight 'o me. "Oh, Mr. Standen, is that you?" she says, all of a pather. "Brooke's not in her bed and we're so dreadfully worried about her. Sir Barnholt told us such things—oh, Mr. Standen, have you seen her?"

"No, Marm, I haven't," says I truly enough. "Last time I peeked in the Garden Room—about an hour since—she were sleeping fair enough."

I noticed Professor Spooner give me an old-fashioned look. "And what are *you* a-doing here, Standen, so late at night?" he starts in to say. But then I see one of the gentlemen with him is Sir Barnholt Weller, as was dad of little Tom what broke his neck. A dentical downright chap, Sir Barney were, with a good headpiece, and a good friend to me, spite of all his trouble.

"Why, it's Sam Standen," he says, kind as can be. "We're main worried about young Brooke, Mr. Standen. Can you help us?"

Seems Sir Barnholt met the Spooners in London, at this-here conference, they got to talking about the house, and what he told them put them in such a frit that they come bustling home directly, 'stead of biding in London overnight as they planned.

"Oh, Mr. Standen, where can she *be*?" says Mrs. Spooner, with the tears a-flowing down. "Where do you think she can have gone?"

"Likely not far, Marm, but 'tis best we hunt quickly," says I, minding me of the lily pool. So we rake that through, all of a quake, but, thanks be, she ain't there, nor up any of the trees nor among the shrubs. Then I bethinks me of the compost heap—which, if I hadn't had my wits dazzled by being woke so sudden, I'd have thought of first. A main big, hot, yeasty heap it be, piled up against the brick wall by the glasshouses. Lawn-grass sweypings, leaves, weeds, and kitchen garbage, all stacked up and up like a layer cake. Wonderful fine compost that do furnish, after two-three years; black as Christmas pudden, it go.

Like I say, I run to the compost heap and, right away, I can see it's been paunched about and bruk up.

"You don't think she can be under *there*—surely, Mr. Standen?" gulps the lady, who's close behind me.

I scoop it up, careful, with my hands; and there, sure enough, she be; buried an arm's-length under, all in among the grass brishings and mixen, and orange peel, and cabbage leaves.

"*Oh God!* She's not dead—is she?" says Mr. Spooner, coming up.

The pile's so sweltering hot, on account o' the fermentation, that the young 'un feels warm as an oven bun and 'tis hard to tell for a minute, but Sir Barnholt feels for her pulse and finds it still going, but terrible slow; half stifled she'd been, under all that gouch. Didn't we got there when we had, she'd not have lived another half hour, says the doctor who had charge of her after the ambulance took her off to hospital. Oxygen, she were given, and needle shots for shock, and her mum and dad half mazed with worry, declaring they'd not spend another week in the house.

For the police had come, and studied the compost heap, and proved that no one except the young one herself had touched it. She'd climbed in and covered herself up, all by her lone, pulling the brishings down on top of her. In her sleep, it was thought. How could they stay in the house where such a thing might happen again?

But young Brooke confounds 'em.

When she comes home, two days after, and hears how they plan to flit, as soon's they can find another place, she fair bursts out crying.

I was there, as it come about.

She was lying out on a sofy under the big cedar and her ma sitting by her as if she'd never take her eyes off again. I happened by with my barrer full of weeds and hear her cry out.

"Move from here? Move *away*? But Ma, little Nym! Poor, poor little Nym! He's my friend! I promised him I'd not leave him!"

"My darling child, how can we stay here? This house is too dangerous for children. And who, tell me, is little Nym?"

Brooke turns to me and says, "Mr. Standen can tell you about little Nym, I bleeve."

So I told the lady. How little Nym was the runt and

weakling of the family, how his elders hated him, on account of he'd been his ma's death. And acos he were ugly and titchy. So they treated him hard and cruel, never played with him or spoke to him; hit and cuffed him and shut him up in cupboards; some days he'd get naught to eat all day. And the famous father had no notion of what were going on; no more notion than if he'd lived in the moon. Never spoke a word to his young 'uns from one week's end to another, by all accounts.

So, one time, accidental-ways, little Nym bust his sister Louisa's pink mug that she set great store by. And they was bound to punish him for that. As it chanced the bishop of Southease was coming to stay at the house, which were a great honor, for their Pa had newly been made a Lord. The other ones were set that young Nym mustn't get to see the bishop, nor his reverince discover they'd such an ugly, puny, marred little brother; accordingly, to hide him away, they buried him in the muckheap and told him he weren't on any account to come out until after the bishop had come and gone. Threatened to wring his neck if he done so.

And the end of it was, at the end of the day, somebody looked for little Nym and found him stifled and dead, under all the muck.

Tarrible scandalized folk were, to find out what had been going on in that fine big house, with so many servants, and the famous father shut away in his study.

"Poor, *poor* little boy," says Miz Spooner, a-wiping her eyes. "But, my honey, you do see why we can't *possibly* stay on here—why, you'd be walking in your sleep again, and little Nym would think up some other dreadful thing to happen to you."

"No, no, Ma," says young Brooke, patient and calm. "Little Nym's my *friend* now. Don't you see? We was there, in the grass heap, so cozy together. And he told me all that happened to him. And I said how sorry I was for him. And I promised I'd be his friend. See: there he is now."

While she talked, she'd been a setting out a dolls' tea service she'd made, from acorn cups and walnut shells and lily pads, on the little table by her sofy. Now she pushes the broken pink mug on a lily pad to the other side of the table, and, says she, "Won't you take a cup of tea, little Nym?"

The

O h yes—I once lived in a hous

the old lady, gazing steadfastl~~~~~~~~~~~~~~~~~ red fire)
—in fact with several ghosts. And they took no
notice of me. It taught me a most painful lesson, one that
I am not likely to forget.

It happened in the year when a great many small local
libraries closed through lack of funds, and a lot of librarians were suddenly looking for jobs. I was one of them.
Middle-aged lady librarians were two-a-penny, and nobody seemed particularly anxious for my services. I have
always been rather solitary, from childhood on, without
friends or relations—I will explain why in a minute; and in
this difficulty I hardly knew where to turn. But fortunately, just at that point, I saw the advertisement in *The
Lady*: "Elderly gentlewoman seeks pleasant Companion
with a predilection for reading aloud."

Now reading aloud has always been one of my greatest
pleasures; first, with my dear mother when we had very

few other resources; and then in Birklethwaite Library, where I ran a regular Reading Circle in the children's section twice a week, for I don't know how many years, and enjoyed it fully as much as any of my listeners.

So I wrote to the Box Number of the elderly gentlewoman, was interviewed, and happily we both took a liking to one another. She was, indeed, a most delightful person, wholly alert, although in her eighties, intelligent and humorous, in appearance a mixture of owl and eagle, with piercing dark eyes, a small beaky nose, and wayward hair standing up on end like white plumes. What she thought of me, I do not know, except that it was sufficiently well to offer me the post, above a number of other applicants; what I thought of *her* was that I should immensely enjoy her company, and probably learn a great deal from her too. It was arranged that I should commence my duties in two months' time.

Mrs. Crankshaw's surroundings were as pleasing as her personality: she lived in a Georgian mansion called Gramercy Place under the slopes of the South Downs, and I looked forward to unlimited walks in the surrounding countryside during my free hours; but to my disappointment, before it was time to take up residence with my new employer, I had a letter informing me of a change of plan.

The poor lady had suffered a slight stroke. "Nothing of consequence, I am already better, apart from being confined, at present, to a wheelchair," she wrote with characteristic firmness, "but I have decided that it would be practical to move to a less solitary environment—better for you, too, my dear Miss Grey. My lawyers are hard at work on the purchase of another house in a small agreeable town—in fact, the purchase of *three* houses which will be converted into one, so that, if we have less outdoors, we shall have plenty of *in*doors, and shall not be on top of one another, which I think is most important. The builders are only waiting for completion to start tearing down partitions, and I trust that our original plans will be put back by no more than a month or two."

She did not mention the name of the small agreeable town, and I waited with interest to learn where it was, confident that our tastes would coincide in this, as they had in other matters.

The purchase went through, but the building work dragged, as such work always does, and it was more like nine weeks before Mrs. Crankshaw was able to transfer herself from the nursing home, and her furniture from Gramercy Place, and write to me that she was ready for me to come and take up my duties in the new residence.

When she did so, the address gave me a shock—the first of several. For she wrote from The Welcome Stranger, Stillingley; and Stillingley was the town where I had spent my childhood, after my father had gone to prison.

And when I reached my destination I received the second shock. For The Welcome Stranger turned out to be the house where my mother and I had lived, now joined together with the houses on either side of it.

"They were all for sale, so I bought the whole little old Tudor row," said Mrs. Crankshaw comfortably. "Luckily my brother's legacy gave me plenty of leeway. (I told you, didn't I, that he had died, and left me some money?) And it is right that the houses should be joined together again, for, apparently, back in the seventeenth century, the whole building was one large inn; only in those days it was called The Bull. But since there is already a Bull Inn in the town, I thought I would choose another old coaching-house name. Besides, it is prettier. The coach entrance was that archway that runs through to the yard at the back."

I could have told her that. I could have told her a great deal more. I had spent thirteen years in that street, in the middle house, and knew every crooked step in it, every beam and cranny, as well as the palm of my own hand. It was wonderful how little the builders had changed; as Mrs. Crankshaw said, the building had been one house two hundred years before; all they needed to do was to knock down a few partitions.

The third and worst shock came as we were having our first cup of tea in the white-paneled parlor—which had been my mother's study where, three days a week, she worked at translation, and read proofs for publishers (on the other three days she had an editorial job on the local paper).

I had asked Mrs. Crankshaw why she picked this particular town, did she have any connections with it?

"Oh yes," she said, tranquilly sipping her Lapsang Souchong. "My brother lived here, in Pallant House, for a number of years. I used to visit him, and always thought it would be a pleasant place in which to settle if, for some unfortunate reason, one was debarred from living out in the real country. My brother was a judge, you may have heard of him: Sir Charles Sydney."

And of course I had heard of him. He was the judge

who had sentenced my father. That was why my mother had moved to the town, after Father had gone to prison. Firstly, we had to give up our own house, we could not afford it. Secondly, visiting would be easier—only an hour's bus ride to the jail where Father was serving his twenty-five-year sentence. But also, having learned, during the trial, that Stillingley was where Sir Charles lived, my mother, apparently at that time, nursed some obscure notion of meeting him in the street or in the Pallant Gardens, or after church on Sunday, and trying to make an appeal to him. "For anyone can see that he is a *good* man," she repeated over and over, with tears in her eyes, "and your father is a good man too; nobody denies that. Somehow, somehow, there *must* be some way of getting his sentence annulled, or at least reduced—I am sure there must be."

But this plan came to nothing, because, firstly, she never ran into Sir Charles or plucked up the courage to approach him. I think he was a very busy man, hardly ever to be seen in the streets of the town, mostly up in London. And, secondly, after serving only two years of the sentence, my father died; of a broken heart, Mother said. I sometimes think it is just as well that he did not live on into the times of *glasnost* and *perestroika* and the end of the Cold War; all that has happened since his conviction makes what he did—sending some not very important scientific information to a colleague in Moscow—seem so pitifully trifling. My father was a civil servant, and of course what he did was strictly forbidden, and counted as treason. But he was a man of tremendously high principles, a pacifist and a conscientious objector; and he felt strongly that all scientific information should be shared equally all over the world. So he was prepared to go to prison for his beliefs. He took himself and his principles to prison; and he left me and Mother out in the cold. Or rather, he left me in prison too . . .

I often thought that he had behaved very unfairly to Mother and me. Either he should not have married and had a family, or he should have chosen some other job. I was only five when he was taken off, and I missed him dreadfully for a number of years. He had been a kind, affectionate father, and used to play lots of games with me. One was called Treasure Islands, a guessing game, trying to find out about each other's treasures; and we told long sagas, each taking up the story in turn; or we did cookery, inventing new dishes from a list of ingredients all beginning with the same letter: apples, anchovies, artichokes, arrowroot . . . Heartburn Holidays, Father used to call those afternoons.

So it was an incurable grief when he vanished away to prison, and a worse one when he died. Mother never married again. She and I reverted to her maiden name of Grey when we moved to Stillingley, because she used to get a lot of hate letters from people who said that Father was a traitor. People seem to have unlimited time for acts of spite to other people who have never done them any personal harm. And about ten years after Father's death, Mother also died. And I took a course in librarianship with the small amount of money she left me, and became a librarian, and worked in libraries for twenty-five years. After Mother's death I never went back to Stillingley. We had no close friends there, because of the quiet life she chose to lead, so it was not at all probable that anybody in the town would recognize me. (Nobody did; partly because the town had changed a great deal. All the little old corner shops had gone, and instead there were tourist boutiques. Walking about the familiar streets, I felt like a ghost myself.)

So, my dears, I expect you can understand why, when Mrs. Crankshaw said, "My brother was a judge: Sir Charles Sydney," I did not at once and honestly exclaim: "Why, he was the judge who sentenced my father to twenty-five years for sending treasonable communications to Soviet Russia," but instead gulped, bit my tongue, knelt to lay another log on the fire, and kept quiet.

Oh, what a difference it would have made if I had not done so! If I had told her that this house was my childhood home. For, once having embarked on a policy of concealment, I was, of course, obliged to go on; there never came an opportunity to change my mind, toss discretion aside, and proclaim: "Oh, by the way, Mrs. Crankshaw, I forgot to mention, when we moved in, that your brother sent my father to prison." That seemed out of the question. And, although I had never in any way blamed her brother—who was only doing his duty, acting on his principles, as Father had acted on his—there was no slightest hint of resentment or anything of that kind—yet, nevertheless, the fact that I was keeping this major secret from her had some kind of crimping or smothering effect on our relationship; happy and friendly although that became.

Well—it *must* have, mustn't it?

But the worst result of all was what I am now going to tell you.

When Mother and I first arrived to live at Middle House, we were busy carrying baskets and jugs and suitcases in through the back door, when I was a little dismayed to observe an eye carefully scanning us from the window of the house next door. And when I say an eye, I mean literally nothing *but* an eye: the bottom left-hand corner of the lace curtain was twitched aside, leaving just room for one muddy gray optic to peer sharply over the window sash and study our possessions.

This gave a decidedly chilly, sinister impression; it could not have been more misleading.

After a day or two spent in getting settled, we began to receive the impression that there was a tremendous amount of back-and-forth, come-and-go, to-and-fro, between the two little houses on either side of us. Upper House, Middle House, and Lower House, the row was called. We occupied Middle House; Upper and Lower Houses appeared to be inhabited by two couples who could not have enough of each other's company. Mr. and Mrs. Brown, Mr. and Mrs. Taylor were their names, we learned from the postman; and we soon discovered why they all lived in one another's pockets—it was because Mrs. Taylor and Mrs. Brown were sisters. In no time at all they had invited us into their highly polished front rooms, resplendent with pot plants and cage birds, and they had given us their life histories. Mrs. Taylor and Mrs. Brown—Di and Ruby—were cockneys, had originally been evacuated to Stillingley in World War I, had fallen in love with local boys, married them, and never returned to London. Their husbands, Fred Taylor and Jim Brown, were, respectively, a bus driver and a builder's foreman. By the end of three weeks, they were playing a very important part in our lives. Fred, every two days, used to bring us fish from Portsbourne, which was at the end of his bus run, and was a monument of sense and experience when it came to practical matters. Jim could deal with any household emergency, could fix leaking taps or loose wiring, mend windows, replace fallen tiles. Ruby and Di supplied the light relief; especially Di. She was a stand-up comic, a harlequin of a woman. Not at all good-looking, she was lean and rangy, with vigorously permed pale-gray locks and skin like uncooked frozen pastry. It was her eye that had peered from under the curtain in Ruby's kitchen. The sisters were perpetually in and out of each other's houses, exchanging pots or clothes, borrowing salt or soap, telling jokes or gossip. "Roo? Are you there, Roo? Got a minute? Come and take a look at this! Di! Got a pinch of bicarb—a few mothballs—a forty-watt bulb—a spoonful of honey?"

Although the husbands had relatives in the town— plenty of them—the two couples formed such a compact group in themselves that they hardly required other company. But they were immensely, infinitely kind to Mother and me. They became our family—surrogate uncles, aunts, grandparents, cousins. "You're so *different* from us!" Di sometimes said wonderingly to Mother. That was because Mother spoke several languages and could translate from German and Russian. Our neighbors themselves

108

had the unassuming modesty, the simple unobtrusive diffidence, of completely happy people. They saw no need to assert themselves; they already had all they required.

It was not long before Mother had told them everything about Father's prison sentence. She had resolved never to mention this circumstance to a single soul in Stillingley; she disclosed it all to Ruby and Di, Jim and Fred, without the least hesitation. She did not even ask for their discretion; she knew by instinct that they would never mention the matter to anybody; and they never did.

They listened to her tale with wondering sympathy, wholly without passing judgment.

"Well: he had to do what he thought right, didn't he?" said Fred.

"And so did the judge; all the same, it does seem a proper shame," said Jim.

"All that time away from you; it's like as if you were a widder," sighed Ruby.

"And poor little Snowball here, so many years without her dad," grieved Di.

From then on they were even kinder to us.

Trip-trap and clitter-clatter through my childhood run the feet of Ruby and Di back and forth outside our dining room window. "Di! Ruby! Listen to this! Can you let me have a lump of dripping? Come and look at the bird, Di! D'you think he's poorly?"

They insisted on our sharing in the products of all their activities: marmalade, chutney, pickled onions.

Soon it was: "Missis Grey? Are you busy? Can you spare a minute?" And quickly the Mrs. Grey gave way to

"Ianthe" (which they shortened to "Ianth"). But, scrupulously, delicately, they never dropped in on my mother during the hours of daylight; Fred, the chieftain of the tribe, had decreed this. "She's the breadwinner, see? You gotta respect that and not go bothering her, you two, mind, while she's workin'."

Fred and Jim, Di and Ruby; they were like the biologist's ideal, a completely self-sufficient society without the need of any outside agency or supplies.

Only once a year, at Christmas, did they summon huge hosts of other relatives, whose arrival was heralded, weeks before, by monumental piles of Christmas cards, which, as soon as they arrived, were slung on zigzag strings across and across the front rooms, in among the cyclamens, the tinsel, poinsettias, mistletoe, and folding paper bells. Then they had a Christmas party. After the first occasion, we carefully avoided those parties, which could last for six, seven, eight hours at a stretch; Mother explained that she really had to go on working over Christmas and could not afford all that time off.

"But what about the liddle 'un? *She* don't have to work."

"She's shy," said Mother firmly.

Those parties did indeed have a numbing, shattering effect, as one munched one's way through more and more sausage rolls and sandwiches, drank more and more lethal mixtures of alcohol and fruit juice, while trying to keep up a continuous fixed smile at the tireless crackle of repartee from cousins, nephews, uncles, and indestructible great-aunts. All these relatives adored and respected our quartet, and would have liked to be invited much more often than once a year. "But we don't want 'em," said Fred, Ruby, Di, or Jim. "We're comfortable just on our loney-own, thank you *very* much—with Ianth and the young 'un."

So time passed for us, peacefully enough; we were buttressed, comforted, and contained by the strong dependable structure on either side.

When I was seven my father died in jail and, during that time, Fred was of silent, sterling support to my mother. He rented a car and drove her to and fro during Father's illness; he drove her to the crematorium, sternly excluding his wife, brother-in-law, and sister-in-law. "No, she don't want you lot; it's a family occasion, see?" And he himself would have stayed outside the chapel if she had not insisted on his coming in, and then he stayed firmly on his own at the back. A surprising number of other people turned up, Mother told me (I was in bed at the time with measles); there were quite a few journalists, and old friends from past days. Mother was glad to dodge them after the ceremony and take refuge with Fred in the rented Rover.

That night my mother and the four neighbors held a kind of wake for Father. I expect she felt she owed it to them; it was what they would have expected. Fruitcake, cold ham, sherry, and whiskey; lying upstairs in bed, feverish, with painfully aching ears and throat, I heard the subdued hum and grumble of voices down below gradually grow more cheerful, an occasional laugh ring out.

"How can they?" I thought, thrashing and tossing in

bed, wretched, sick, and furious. Fred came up with a jug of lemonade and found me so, tears hissing on my hot red cheeks like water on the surface of an iron.

I glared at him, kept by manners and convention from saying what I felt.

But he understood perfectly well.

"I know, I know," he said, settling his stocky bulk down with caution on my cane-seated chair. "You think we're all heartless down there, don't you, tellin' jokes to your mum and makin' her laugh? But she's done a deal of sorrowin' already, and she's got a deal more to do; she needs a bit of a break. It ain't unfair to your dad; I expect he'd do the same. I daresay he liked a bit of a laugh in his time, didn't he? I expect he told you a good few jokes?"

Reluctantly I nodded.

"Well then," said Fred. "Just you remember, dearie; death ain't all black plumes and caterwauling. You got to carry on as best you can."

Fred saw us through various other troubles. When our cat died, he helped bury her; when my first boyfriend dropped me, left me a stricken thirteen-year-old grass widow, he managed to make me believe there were as good fish in the sea, which helped at the time, though in fact he was wrong, for I never acquired another.

And then, when I was fifteen, Di died. She had been growing gradually thinner and more gaunt; there was less vivacity in her jokes. She underwent an operation; spent painful weeks in bed at home, tended by Mother and Ruby. Then Fred said to me one day: "I've got to tell you this fast—we're going to lose her," and bolted blindly out of our kitchen. He himself was losing weight at a rapid rate; after her death he became, suddenly, a shrunken thread of a man. Ruby and Jim took him into their house, as they said he shouldn't be on his own. By this time I was sixteen, about to go off on a residential course at the other end of England. Fred was in bed, ill, when I left; I kissed him goodbye and never saw him again. Jim soon followed; it was as if, once the structure and symmetry of the group had been damaged, its individual members were vulnerable, badly at risk. Jim died of bronchitis, coughing his lungs away. He had been a heavy smoker. Poor Ruby could not bear her life without the others around her.

"It just don't seem right," she said to Mother. She developed a heart trouble and died in the ambulance on the way to the hospital. Now the houses on either side of us were up for sale; and one day, at my residential college, I received a telegram to say that my mother had died of pneumonia, very suddenly, in the local hospital. Like Ruby, she was unable to manage without the rest of the group to support her.

After letting Middle House for a couple of years, to support me through my training, I sold it, having no wish to return there. New neighbors were installed on either side. The thought of Upper House without Fred and Di, of Lower House without Jim and Ruby, of our own house without my mother, was not to be borne, I would have felt like a survivor from a holocaust. I found a plain job elsewhere, in a plain library in a plain provincial town, and entrenched myself in books, catalogs, indexes, and reading aloud.

Until the day, over twenty years later, when I found

113

myself back there, installed in The Welcome Stranger, with Mrs. Crankshaw.

She, in her wheelchair, professed herself wholly delighted with the three houses fashioned into one. The builders had made ramps for her, so that her domain was entirely on the ground floor, bedroom at one end, living space in the middle, kitchen at the other. So her living quarters were constructed from Mother's and my old kitchen–dining room, where Ruby and Di had clattered continually past the window. Her bedroom was Ruby's front room, where the terrifying Christmas parties had taken place. I could sit reading *Dr. Thorne* aloud to Mrs. Crankshaw and think of all those spangled cards fluttering overhead, and Fred's nephew Peter rolling his eyes under the mistletoe. My bedroom was upstairs (my own old bedroom, as it fell out), and there I lay at night, listening to the house creak and rustle gently round me; Mrs. Crankshaw had installed gas-fired central heating.

After a few weeks, Mrs. Crankshaw said to me, "Miss Grey—Lucy—I am quite delighted with this house, and with our arrangement; I hope that you are too? But would you say—entirely without prejudice—that the place is slightly haunted?"

"No one has said anything of the kind to me, Mrs. Crankshaw," I fenced.

"Oh, won't you call me Moira, my dear, don't you think we have reached that stage by now? No, of course I had no such intimation from the agents or the lawyers or the builders—but then, one never does, does one? Just the same, I do begin to wonder. During the last twenty years there seem to have been a great many occupants. Do you think it was because no one cared to stay very long?"

It was true that, since the time of Jim and Ruby, Fred and Di and my mother, the three little houses had changed hands repeatedly. Nobody seemed to have stayed more than a year or so.

"But that need not mean a thing," I argued, quite truly. "The whole town is in a—a state of transition. House prices are rising so fast, people buy them as investments, do them up, and move on. Also, the place is becoming more of a tourist center than it—than it probably was twenty years ago."

It was becoming harder and harder to maintain my pretense of never having lived in the town before. I felt worse and worse about it. Because our relationship—Moira's and mine—was, in all other respects, so happy, open, and free; she was beginning to seem like a beloved aunt, or cherished older sister; one of those relations I had never been blessed with. We were able to talk to one another about every possible topic—except one; and our reading-aloud sessions were periods of calm, undiluted pleasure.

"What is giving you the idea that the place might be haunted?" I asked with caution.

"Why, there are times—especially when you are reading to me, my dear—when I am almost convinced that I can hear *voices*—voices perhaps in the next room, or somewhere else about the house, or perhaps in the little lane at the back."

"Perhaps they are real voices?" I suggested hopefully. "Echoes, you know, from the lane."

A CREEPY COMPANY

The little lane—along which Ruby and Di used to run to and fro all day—was a right-of-way and led to the public library, my long-ago haunt of comfort and instruction.

"Well, yes, sometimes they might be real," agreed Mrs. Crankshaw, "but not always. Not late at night. And the voices inside the house *must* be ghosts—mustn't they? Unless I am going potty."

"And that you certainly are not, dear Mrs. Crankshaw," I said fervently.

"Moira, my dear—Moira." Her hawk-eyes gleamed.

"What *kind* of voices do you think you hear?"

"You are sure you don't hear them yourself?" she inquired wistfully.

"No, I'm afraid I don't. Not at present. Perhaps I shall, by and by."

Oh, how I wished this! For she said, "Well, there are several different voices. That's why I'm sure it can't be just my imagination—for I never was very imaginative, you know, even as a child, I was the most prosaic little creature, and never cared particularly for pretend games or fairy stories. How could I invent something like this? What I hear is most often women's voices—quite raucous and cheerful, with a cockney twang to them. Not a bit like our good neighbors up and down the hill."

The good neighbors up and down the hill were nearly all antique dealers, who went in for a good deal of packaged refinement and ersatz chumminess; the females wore tweeds, and the males neatly trimmed beards.

"And you hear the voices particularly when I am reading to you?"

"Yes, is that not curious? It is precisely like—you know

116

when you tune into a radio station, and at first it comes through, perfectly clear, and then, by degrees, some foreign station comes in and jams it; though that is not quite the case here, for I can always hear you, my dear Lucy, perfectly well—but then in the background the voices begin."

"Always women's?"

"No; the women are the most frequent, but occasionally I get male voices farther back—two different ones, I am fairly sure, one quite deep-toned and gruff, the other higher and more nasal."

"Can you hear what they *say*?" I asked with quivering interest.

"Not yet, my dear. But let us hope that in due course I shall! Really, nothing so interesting has happened to me for years—and I am sure that I owe it all to your company in this pleasant place, my dear Lucy; I am so very happy that we had the luck to find each other."

Her words filled me with mingled guilt and relief. Relief that she appeared to be deriving so much pleasure and interest from the phenomenon; many old ladies might have felt very differently; guilt that it was too late for me to be more candid and forthcoming about my friends; I felt I was doing them serious injustice by not telling her all about them.

Oh, what a tangled web we weave! . . .

While Mrs. Crankshaw kept exclaiming in her satisfaction at what a warm, welcoming atmosphere the place had—"Just like its name! I christened better than I knew!"—I, perhaps because I found myself in such a curious moral dilemma, felt the house curiously cold and unresponsive. No echoes came back to me, not a sound, not a signal, from the happy childhood hours I had passed there. And some of them *had* been happy: moments of hope, before my father died; moments of peace and companionship when my mother and I read aloud *Villette* or *War and Peace* in late-spring evenings with a pale moon looking solemnly in at my bedroom window; moments of triumph when I had done well at school; or moments of pure fun when Di and Ruby were clowning and Fred and Jim, with us, were laughing at them.

I could not escape the impression that the house was displeased with me. I should have come clean; and I had not.

Mrs. Crankshaw began to have remarkable dreams.

"I see such faces! Such real characters! Can they be people whom I have met, at some point during my life, and completely forgotten? They seem so extremely real. There is one extraordinary woman—a tall, bony, angular creature, with false teeth, and such a laugh! I have dreamed about her several times. Her name is Vi or Di—something like that. I must say, she is very entertaining. I wonder if I can be developing mediumistic powers in my old age? I must talk to the vicar about it."

She talked to the vicar, but he was new and young, and come to the town long since the days of Fred and Jim and Ruby and Di. He could make nothing of Mrs. Crankshaw's dreams. He assured us that, so far as he knew, nobody had experienced anything of this kind in the house.

I thought, also, that Mrs. Crankshaw might be developing mediumistic powers. Was what was happening a kind of telegraphic flash passing over from my memory to hers? Was she picking up scenes from my past—my carefully suppressed past—and, as it were, printing them off in the darkroom of her mind? Did she see these things because I was there?

Or was she receiving entirely new impressions? Were the ghosts of Jim and Fred, of Di and Ruby, still floating around, still present in the house—disturbed, perhaps, by my arrival, by the builders' work—available to Mrs. Crankshaw because she was so happily, generously ready to receive them—but not choosing to reveal themselves to me?

That was indeed a chilling thought.

I could imagine—all too easily—Fred's quarterdeck voice. (He had been a petty officer once, long ago, before he retired from the navy and took to bus driving.) I remembered how sternly he had said: "She's the breadwinner, see? You gotta respect that and not go bothering her, you two." I imagined him saying: "You shoulda told the lady the whole story, Snowball, right from the start. Now you put yourself in what they call a false position. And you put *us* in one too."

Oh how I longed to apologize, to confess, to have matters somehow set right!

One morning Mrs. Crankshaw called to me, in a voice of pure astonishment:

"Lucy! Somebody pushed my wheelchair!"

Contrary to her hopes, she had never recovered the use of her legs; her upper body was active, but below her hips she was motionless. Because of the ramps, all the ground floor of the house was accessible to her; she had a self-propelled wheelchair with an inner and an outer wheel.

She could spin herself around, very easily, through her downstairs domain, and did so, all day long. It was only when we went out of doors that I pushed her. But the wheelchair had a self-activating brake, a locking device which automatically engaged when the chair came to rest, so that it could never accidentally roll.

"Somebody," said Mrs. Crankshaw, with absolute conviction, "*some*body disengaged the brake and pushed me over to the front window."

"You are quite sure that you didn't, almost unconsciously, do it yourself?"

She thought about it. "No, my dear. Because my tiresome old fingers are growing so arthritic and stiff these days that, when I heard a horse's hoofs go clopping past outside, I did just wonder, would it be worth unlocking the brake and rolling myself over to take a look out of the window. But I decided not to bother—and then, you see, some kind agency did it for me!"

I felt—believe it or not—a prickle of jealousy.

I said, "Dear Mrs. Crankshaw. I am so very sorry about your hands. Let me give them a rub with liniment. And you know that, wherever I am about the house, if you give me a call, I'll always *gladly* come and move your chair—"

"Oh, my dear, I know you will! And my hands are nothing—a trifle. With so few disabilities, in this charming house and with your company, I am a very lucky old person. And now, it seems, I have a friendly ghost to push me about as well."

She laughed with real pleasure.

But I felt nervous. Bitterly ashamed, of course—for how could I possibly mistrust my kind friends enough to suppose that they might do Mrs. Crankshaw any harm? Just the same, from then on, I kept a very sharp eye on the position of her chair, and would casually move stools or small tables into its possible path, so that it could never roll very far.

Several times, during the next few weeks, the chair was moved again, always to anticipate some vague wish that Mrs. Crankshaw had hardly yet expressed, even to herself. "They positively forestall my needs," she said, laughing. "It really is *most* interesting, my dear Lucy. I am so *sorry* that you can't see them."

For now she was beginning to get a glimpse of them—in odd, short flashes.

"Rather like a flickering, faulty television screen," was how she expressed it. "And, yes, sometimes in color, sometimes black-and-white. Color comes most often at twilight—black-and-white during full daylight. At night they seem to fade completely—just the reverse of what one expects of ghosts."

Bit by bit, she described them.

"There is the tall, rangy woman. These are all quite modern specters, my dear. No ruffs, or crinolines, or nonsense of that kind. The tall woman wears high-heeled leather kneeboots and a long narrow tube of a skirt, with an apron over it, and layers and layers of cardigans. Very often she has her hair in curlers. She is always the strongest image. Then there is a shorter woman, who nearly always has a piece of knitting in her hand."

Dear Ruby! The number of hideous fancy-stitch sweaters she had knitted me, which I was obliged out of politeness (and need also) to wear until I had outgrown them.

"Then there is a stocky thickset man who wears a dark-blue uniform. Perhaps he is a postman? I get a feeling of great kindness and dignity. And a little gnomelike fellow who spends hours poring over a folded-up square inch of newspaper, and always has a cigarette dangling from his lip. He is the faintest of them—but still, he is growing clearer as the days go by."

"Just those four? No others?"

No gray-haired, thin-faced woman with horn-rimmed glasses, busy at her typewriter?

"No, you greedy creature," said Mrs. Crankshaw, laughing. "Aren't four well-constructed honest-to-goodness spooks enough for you? *How* I wish my dear brother Charles were still alive; he used to be such a skeptical materialist, would never admit even the possibility of ghosts. What a good time I should have, telling him about mine! I really begin to feel as if they were my own family—my family of phantoms."

To hear her say that gave me a terrible twinge. And then she began to speak of writing to the *Psychic News.* "This is such an interesting phenomenon, my dear. I feel it should be shared with experts."

"But," I argued, "then they would want to come down and inspect and investigate, and put in watchers and try to take pictures with infrared light—or however people do photograph ghosts; do you really want all that going on in your peaceful house?"

She glanced round the pleasant white-paneled parlor.

"Well, no," she conceded. "Perhaps not."

In fact, to me, the house was *not* peaceful any longer. It seemed to throb with reproof and reproach. I knew that the time had come when I must, I absolutely must confess all, and make a clean breast to Mrs. Crankshaw.

And what a poor figure I was going to cut! Deceitful, dishonest, hypocritical, cowardly, dishonorable—but, above all, shabby and perfidious to my good friends. Was it so surprising that they seemed to have turned against me?

I decided to make my confession one evening, after our reading-aloud period, between tea and supper. That was our easiest, happiest time, when we were most completely in tune with one another; then, I thought, I would have the best chance of winning forgiveness and understanding from Mrs. Crankshaw for my long course of deceit.

All day my heart rattled painfully inside my rib cage. Mrs. Crankshaw occupied herself as usual, in reading newspapers and political journals, in writing letters to her bed-bound friends, with sketching and solitaire and petit-point; she was a most self-sufficient person. Occasionally she would raise her eyes from the card table or embroidery pillow to remark, "There goes the tall lady past the window, carrying a birdcage with a canary in it. Do canaries have ghosts too, poor little things?" Or, "Now I see the man in blue. He is carrying one of those rush baskets that fish used to be sold in; do you remember them? Do ghosts eat fish?"

Oh Fred, I thought. He would be bringing the fish for my mother and me. Oh dear, *dear* Fred, why can't I see you too? I'll tell her this very evening. The minute that we have finished our stint on *Wuthering Heights*. And then perhaps, perhaps they will show themselves to me.

We had our reading session, installed as usual: Mrs. Crankshaw on the sofa, comfortably snugged in, with cushions behind her and a rug over her knees; myself in the rocker with the table lamp at my side. Twilight was falling fast.

I read aloud several chapters. We were very close to the end.

"Shall I stop here?" I said nervously, clearing my throat.

"Oh no, *do* go on, my dear—if you are not becoming hoarse? Do finish the book. I don't know *how* many times I have read *Wuthering Heights*," said Mrs. Crankshaw with satisfaction. "And it gets better every time."

"Are you—are you hearing the voices?" I asked.

"Just a little. They are chatting comfortably in the background. Not intrusively, you know—but like people in the next room who know that we shall stop our reading and talk to them by and by."

So I read on; read the last two chapters, came to the last line: "*I wondered how anyone could ever imagine unquiet slumbers for the sleepers in that quiet earth.*"

Closing the book, I let a silence of a few moments elapse. The room was almost dark now, apart from the bright circle of my reading light. I glanced about—hoping for a glimpse of a long tube skirt, a head of curlers, a pair of leather kneeboots, a dark-blue uniform jacket. But there was nothing.

"Mrs. Crankshaw: there is something I have to tell you.

Something I should have told you long ago, at the very beginning of our friendship. *Listen:—*"

But I had left it too late.

Mrs. Crankshaw's head had fallen back peacefully on her cushion; her hands, relaxed, lay open on the rug. She had gone for good, and left me all alone in that silent, silent house.

Die from Day to Day

It seemed to him that he was a middle-aged man, tired and irritable, beset by many cares, both professional and domestic, driving his family back along the highway. It seemed they had been spending a short and acrimonious vacation at a Joplins Super-Holiday Theme Park in Bridpool. Fun for the Kids, Relaxation for the Adults. Neither promise had been kept. The kids, three girls, had been bored, the adults had quarreled. The hope had been that this vacation would repair their tottering marriage. The hope had withered on the stem.

"Can't you drive a bit faster, Ewart?" his wife cried impatiently. "We've had a rotten week, we might as well get home while the shops are open. And the girls still have their vacation homework to do."

His response was to drop his speed by five miles an hour. Eva pressed her lips together in fury, but kept silent. After a few minutes he said, sourly, "Why didn't they bring their homework with them?"

"Oh, Ewart! They did bring it, but there was never any time. Or any place to do it."

Casting his mind back, with reluctance, among the small circular glass tables scattered here and there in the purple-carpeted lounge areas, through the ever-howling storm of music, through the clattering crowded ranch-style eaterie, the comfie coffeeteria, the bun-burger bakerie, and the solaroid sports salon, he was obliged to admit that what she said was no more than the truth. The children's bedroom had been simply a sleep area, with small basin and three-tiered bunk; the adult bedroom merely a space containing emperor-sized bed, obsessionally frilled, a tea tray on legs, shower cabinet, and TV screen; the notion of work, reading or writing, was neither entertained at that place nor catered for.

"Vacations were different when I was a boy," he muttered, half to himself. "We did a lot of reading. We kept diaries."

"Oh, Dad! You and your Good Old Days. Always on about them."

"They *were* good," he asserted grumpily. "I'm telling you, if I were to be offered one day—just *one* day—from any one of those childhood holidays, I'd accept it even if it meant living through all the rest of my life over again. And that's saying something!"

"It certainly is," his wife commented dryly. "I wouldn't live through *my* life over again, not for the Golden Apples of the Whatdoyoucallem. Not for anything you could offer me."

Her voice was loaded with venom.

127

The girls in the back were, by now, as usual, scuffling over some toy. Voices were raised in dispute.

"Mine!"

"No, mine!"

"Ma, Lecky's gone and ruined it. She's broken it!"

"I like that. It was you who lost the washer!"

"Tish had the washer. She put it in her pocket."

"Well, I haven't got it now. You took it, Lecky."

"Oh, do be quiet, all of you!" shouted their father. "Or I'll stop the car and dump you all out on the side of the highway."

"You couldn't *do* that!"

"You're not allowed!"

"It's illegal!"

"Quiet, girls, when your father tells you," said Eva, but without conviction, and she distributed cookies, which produced a munching silence for a few minutes, followed by demands for drinks.

"We just passed the last service area," said Ewart. "There isn't another for forty miles."

He felt a sour satisfaction in being able to thwart them so completely.

"Should have filled the flask before we started. Or brought some juice."

The children returned to their wrangle about the washer, and he, to distract his thoughts from the disagreeable present, went back to the past.

Where had it been, that childhood paradise? North, east, or west? He had no idea. Memory had no clues to offer. There had been a stone-built cottage, slate-roofed; a sandy, pebbled turnaround for the car, a brook with a footbridge, a ford, through which the car had to splash. On some joyful occasions, when there had been heavy rain higher up the valley, they were marooned at the cottage until the water level went down. There was a rocky river, a gravel-bed, a pinewood, a heather-covered hillside. There were trout in the river, owls at night, hares in the meadows. Mushrooms, found in dewy dawns. Hazelnuts, found in bird-haunted thickets.

There had been a companion who played with him, in the beechwoods, on the gravel-bed, building palaces, in the river, wading and jumping from rock to rock, swimming, retiring to the haybarn when it rained.

What had been her name?

She had been *the* companion, the perfect one, setting a standard, ideal, irrevocable, to which no one else could ever aspire; the prototype, the archetype, the paragon, the unattainable summit.

No other person, ever again, whether male or female, had supplied that perfection of fellowship.

What was her name? Who was she, where had she come from?

"Oh, do be quiet!" he cried to his quarreling daughters. "Read your books, for heaven's sake, can't you? I've got a lot to worry about without your constant row."

"*Worrying* won't help," said Eva disagreeably.

"I like that!" he snapped at her. "You'll have to suffer too, you'll all suffer, if the case goes against me and I have to pay out thirty thousand to that woman. Money doesn't grow on trees."

"It doesn't grow on trees for *her*, either. Poor devil. After all, it was you who ran over her husband."

129

"He was drunk! Blotto! Falling about in the road like a bagatelle ball. It's just astonishing something of the kind hadn't happened to him months ago, years ago."

"It was just his bad luck that all the other drivers but you managed to avoid him," said Eva. The girls had stopped quarreling to listen. "And now that poor woman is left to bring up her children on her own."

Was that a note of envy in her voice?

The highway went snaking along, through empty country, between highish wooded hills, brownish blue, bluish-brown, humped one behind the other, their outlines beginning to soften in the gathering dusk. There was very little other traffic at this time, at this season.

"And what about the other case?" said his wife. "When is that due to come to court?"

Now her voice definitely held a note of malicious amusement.

Ewart kept quiet, went on driving. One of the girls said: "What other case, Ma?"

"Your father was so unfortunate as to wall a poor old lady up, alive, in her own house."

"He did what?"

"Oh, rubbish, Eva. What terrible rubbish you talk," he said angrily. "It was nothing like that, and you know it. You might at least not take pains to put the children against me, give them entirely erroneous ideas—"

"What happened, Ma? Tell us!"

"Damn it, Eva, I was only the council planning officer—you make it sound as if I, personally, boarded her up—"

"Ma, what happened?"

"If you ever looked at the papers you'd know about it," said Ewart sharply, pulling out into the fast lane to over-take a truck that said EQUINE AND BOVINE REMOVALS. PASS WITH CARE.

"Well," said Eva, "there was this poor old widow lady, Mrs. Murchison, and she'd got so old that she couldn't look after herself very well. She didn't *want* to leave her house, but the Council decided that she should go into Sheltered Accommodation, where she would be looked after by a warden, and her house, which had got into a very run-down state because it hadn't been re-paired, or done over, for years and years, should be pulled down.

"So one department of the Council was to come and fetch the old lady, with her things, in an ambulance, and take her away to the Sheltered Accommodation. And an-other department, later on, was to come and board up the windows of the house, and nail up the doors, until the demolition people came to knock it down."

"Why couldn't they do that at the same time?"

"That sort of thing always takes a long time to arrange. Don't ask me why."

"So what happened?"

"Oh, do be *quiet*, Eva!"

"What happened," went on Eva, taking no notice of her husband's protest, "was that the people from the Council got their dates the wrong way round. The board-ing-up crew came to the house a month before the ambu-lance crew. And they didn't hear old Mrs. Murchison, who was very weak, letting out a few wails and squeaks from where she lay on the sofa in the back kitchen. They

131

nailed up the door and they boarded up the windows. And it wasn't until the ambulance people came, a month later, that anybody realized anything was wrong."

"Was she dead?" asked one of the children, awestruck.

"Indeed she was. But perhaps," remarked Eva pensively, "she really would have preferred it that way. Perhaps she'd rather die in her own home—even if it was a bit dark and stuffy, with no view out of the windows—perhaps she'd prefer that to being wheeled off against her will in an ambulance."

"I wouldn't," said one of the girls.

"Be quiet, Lecky! How can you tell what you'd like?"

"If it was me, I'd sooner swallow some pills."

"Ah, but perhaps you wouldn't have the pills to swallow. How can you tell she had?"

"Perhaps she was too weak to walk as far as the bathroom."

Trying to ignore the chatter, Ewart plunged back into the past.

The river had been brown, the color of amber, sliding along over its pebbles. Where it deepened to a ten-foot pool, deep enough to dive into from a rock, there it was darker in color, like brown ale, or stout, but so clear that you could see right to the bottom, see the sandy bed, and the fish lurking. On the gravel-bed there were quartz stones, purple, white and pink. Up on the moor there were Roman remains to be found, as well as traces of earlier, ancient men, Pictish settlements and stone circles.

They had walked and walked for miles, they had ridden bicycles, they had climbed steep honey-scented rocky hillsides.

What was her name, she, the companion, lost, inaccessible, irrevocably gone?

Was it because of her that all other women, ever since, had seemed so petty, spiteful, dull, antagonistic?

What bliss the return had been, every summer, to find the place unchanging, unchanged. The same in every slightest particular, the little wooden footbridge spanning the brook, the gravel track, the shallow ford. Always they followed the same ritual on arrival, the children would leap from the backseat of the car and ride through the ford standing on the running board. In those days cars had running boards. The water would rise in a curved crest on either side but leave them dry. And then, ahead, there lay the cottage, solid, ancient, gray, against its protecting trees and outbuildings. And old Annie to greet them joyfully with their favorite supper. And after supper she would bath them in the oval zinc tub, in the little lean-to washhouse. And during the bathing process she would tell them stories, of Scath the Warrior Queen, of the Ninth Wave, of the Death Weaver at the Pole, or the Three Marvels of Hy. But their favorite of all was the tale of the Bean Nighe, the Washer of the Ford. "Tell about the Bean Nighe, Annie! Please!"

"She stands upon the banks of the stream. The banks have mist and shadow. She has her back turned, always her back turned. And she is washing and slapping at the linen, great ropes of white linen that she lifts from the waters, lifts and drops into the water, lifts again and beats on the stones to cleanse the cloth. And, as the dirt falls from the linen into the waters, so the woman sings and croons: 'O arone, aree, eily arone, arone! O, O, arone, eily arone!' And thus she stands among the shadows as the days come and go, the months come and go, the years come and go."

"But tell what happens, Annie, if she sees you!"

"All is well if you can slip past the woman, slip across the ford as she washes her linen, if you can slip past behind her back without her seeing you, and go on your way. But O, woe, if she should chance to turn and see you, for her face is so terrible that none can bear the sight of it, and she will strike at you in her anger, scream and slap at you with the weight of the heavy wet linen. And then, and then, O woe betide you!"

"What happens, what happens to you, Annie?"

"The Washer will put your death on you, from that day forward your death is upon you, and you will groan with the weight of it. For you will die from hour to hour, and you will die from day to day. Never a moment's peace will you have, from the time when she sets her terrible eyes upon you and strikes at you with the fearsome weight of the wet linen that she holds in her bony hand.

"Now, off with ye, get to bed with ye, the pair of ye."

And she would chase them upstairs to bed, and all night long the voice of the river, its rustle and murmur, would come through the open casement and be in their ears and in their thoughts and lull them into dreams.

"So, what did they do," cried the girls in the back, "what did they do with the old lady in the house, did they bury her?"

"Of course they buried her, stupid, they wanted to pull down the house, didn't they? They took her out and buried her. The Council did that. But there had to be an inquest first."

"Didn't she have any family? Anybody to worry about her?"

"Only a nephew. And he was in New Zealand."

"Oh, do be *quiet*. Or talk about something else," Ewart called to the girls in the back.

"But it's interesting, Daddy. What will they do to you, because of it? Will they send you to prison?"

"Of course they won't do that, children," interposed his smiling wife. "Daddy was only the planning officer, that's not a very important position. But perhaps he will be asked to resign. Or there'll be an inquiry, but they often take a very long time, and don't prove anything."

"What about the man that Daddy ran over? Won't he be sent to prison for that?"

"No, no, the coroner said the man was a risk to the public and to himself."

"So why does his wife want Daddy to pay her all that money?"

"Because thirty years ago he was a well-known singer," said Tish patiently. "Everybody but you knows *that*. He used to make money once, singing his songs, and now his wife won't have that to live on."

"That's not fair. He might just as well have been a street cleaner."

"Well," said Eva lightly, "it will teach your father to drive more carefully from now on, won't it?"

All of a sudden, Ewart swerved the car onto the shoulder and switched off the motor.

"Daddy! What's the matter? What are you doing? Have you run out of gas? Why are you getting out?"

"What is it, Ewart? Have you got backache?"

Eva's voice was mocking, only mildly concerned.

"No. This is where I quit. You can take on the driving. You can take the kids home. There's enough in the tank to get you to Ambley Service Station."

"Ewart! What do you *mean*?"

"Daddy! *Daddy!*"

But he was already scrambling down the bushy, brambly embankment, he was deaf to the shock and fright in their shrill voices.

She can drive them, he muttered to himself, over and over. She's often told me she's a better driver than I am. Now she can jolly well take over.

There was a high barbed-wire fence at the foot of the bank; he pushed through it, regardless of rips to his jacket and trousers.

And then he was in the woods.

By now it was gathering dusk. Through sloe-bushes and hawthorn, ahead of him, he could see larger trees, and the shape of the round hills, curving on either side. The wooded landscape was silent; perhaps the weather was too cold and too gray for birds to be engaged in their evening chorus. But there was a fresh, wet, cold scent everywhere, a cold northern smell of true country, very different from the stale, used air which hung about the tennis courts and golf-links of Joplins Super-Holiday Theme Park. He could smell mud, and fungus, and rotten wood, and crushed nettles.

For miles on miles, it seemed, he fought his way through the intractable woodland without ever chancing on a footpath. It seemed as if no human beings ever made use of this land. Deer trails there were, sometimes, or rabbit tracks, but they soon petered out. Yet he struggled on, instinctively keeping a course, walking in a northerly direction. And by degrees the trees, ash and beech, began to give way to smaller ones, alder and wild plum, and these to blackberry clumps; and at last he came out on a grassy hillside, looking down into a valley.

It seemed to him that the contours of this valley were very familiar. By instinct, he turned right, going eastward, and soon came to a drystone wall, and climbed it. Now, downhill, before him, ran a road, straight as a rule, switchbacking over a series of ridges, making its way directly to the valley bottom. He followed, and he recognized every bush along the way, every clump of broom, every mossy rock on the bank at either side.

If there were voices behind him, at the top of the hill, crying faintly in the twilight wind, he took no notice. Women! he thought, a pack of women, clamoring always at my heels, young and old, clamoring for attention, for money, for things I can't give them, and don't want to give them. The old girl boarded up in the house, the woman whining on about her sot of a husband, Eva, sneering and unsatisfied, the girls yapping after me, day after day, like penny Furies.

I'm happy to be quit of them, and hope I never hear any of their voices, ever again.

At the foot of the hill the way divided, and this, too, he

remembered. The tarred road swung right, and a sandy pebbled track led off to the left, downhill, between banks of pale, tussocky grass. This was his way.

Dusk lay about him now, in layers of cold shadow, and it did not seem to him at all strange that, though he had walked for hours now as it seemed, still this same twilight had been about him ever since he left the motorway. It had never grown much darker. It was like the Arctic summer twilight, that lasts all night.

He came to a sharp turn in the lane, and now, ahead, he could hear the twofold music of the brook and the river; the brook a light, bubbling chuckle, near at hand; the river a deeper, louder murmur, the distance of a wide meadow farther on.

He turned a corner of the tussocky bank, and there was the wooden footbridge. And he saw the shallow ford, and the pebbly slope above it, leading up to the ancient gray cottage, snug among its trees.

And he saw something else.

He saw a woman, clothed in gray, stooping, with her ankles in the shallow water, and a great white mass of woven stuff that she dragged upward, and shook and pummeled and dropped into the brook again, as if it were a painful, deadly weight to her, and yet she must perform this action, keep performing it, forever, perhaps. So she stooped, and rose, and worked at her heavy task in the cold gloaming, as if she had been at it since the beginning of the world, through back-breaking ages, and must continue to do it for as many ages to come. And, as she stooped and wrought, and worked and wrung at the linen, she chanted mournful words: "Arone! Aree! O, O, eily arone."

And the shadows gathered round her.

Now it seemed to Ewart that, since she was so deeply engrossed in her strange occupation, and her melancholy song, there might be a chance for him to creep past her across the bridge. For cross it he must, if he were ever to reach the house where he longed to be.

So, with his heart in his mouth, he crept, step by step, toward the water. Now he was perilously close to the strange Washer at her endless task; but still he began to think that he might be able to creep by unseen.

And then, all of a sudden, round she swung, and, O, the look she gave him!

"So it is *you*, is it?" she said, with her terrible eyes on him. "O indeed, and it is a long time I've been waiting for you, Ewart of the pale cheek! Well I remember how in the old days you would pull my hair and pinch my wrist, how you took the ball that was mine, and the arrow that I had made, because it had a better point, how you filled my cup with sand, how it was always you, because you were a boy, that had the better portion of meat or honey bread, how you pushed my head under in the water and stamped on my toes in the hay barn. O, and indeed you have a score to answer for, Ewart my old playmate, my onetime companion!"

And, lifting the heavy cold mass of her linen out of the brook, she struck him with it, one freezing, stinging blow across the face, which made him reel and gasp and clutch at the air with his hands.

"Mercy! Mercy!" he besought her. "I only wanted—I only wanted—"

But the gray house was fading away into the shadows; fading fast; and now it had vanished entirely.

"What you want," said she, "is not to be had. Is never to be had! And now the doom is on you, and you must go back, step by painful step, the way you came. And you will groan with the weight that is laid upon you. And you will die from day to day."

And that was how it was.

Fastness of Light

"I expect you were pleased to get such a good degree?" one of the women on the interviewing board said kindly.

I muttered an inaudible reply.

"That's hardly the point, is it?" one of the men grunted. "Point is, can she ride a bicycle?"

"Yes I can," I said. Stupid with fright, the last thing I wanted was to have to use my wits, and the thought of riding a bicycle forever across a flat landscape was infinitely soothing.

The board dismissed me, after firing at me a few questions in French, which I had claimed to be able to speak. In a week or so I learned that I had been granted a position in the filing section of the pensions department of this large government office.

The filing section of the pensions department was housed in a large mansion out in the country, called Holm Hall. It had once been a farm, but in the middle of the

nineteenth century had been bought by the retired manu-
facturer of Judd's Ginger Beer, who remolded it to his
taste, giving it two new wings, a ballroom, a musicians'
gallery, and a tower.

Here, fairly soon, I went, to experience a sharper
wretchedness than I have ever known at any time since
then. It was winter when I arrived at Holm Hall, a particularly bleak, black, endless winter. Patches of frozen snow
lay in the garden and the ground was baked by cold to a
hard, rutted crust. Everything about the house filled me
with horror: the impossibly high varnished pine doors and
windows, the immense areas of freezing polished floor,
the light, shiny, elaborate paneling. It seemed as if no one
could ever be at home in such a place—had ever been at
home.

I was taken straight away to the clerks' room, brightly
lit, full of the smell of red-hot stove. Here sat Miss Vosper, Miss Danby, Miss Craw, Miss Lark, Miss Heatherly,
Miss Jones, Miss Bishop, Miss Kidnell. All of them were
old, they looked at me gloomily and malevolently, and I
could see that they were determined, one and all, to take
no sauce from me. Not that I had any intention of proffering sauce; far from it.

Miss Vosper, head of the department, began instructing
me in my duties. Twice a day I was to take the mail on my
bicycle to the village post office; I was to stick the stamps
on the envelopes, and keep a record of letters sent in the
postbook. I was shown where the bicycle was kept, and
with a sigh of relief I set off carrying the afternoon's batch
of outgoing letters. The road to the village plunged verti-

cally down from Holm Hall and the brakes on the bicycle were far from efficient; the descent was fraught with anxiety. And on the return journey I wondered if it was worth using a bicycle at all, since it had to be pushed all the way. But at least I could balance the parcels, marked "On Her Majesty's Service," on the saddle.

As I walked, pushing the bike, through the large gates, a voice from behind startled me.

"Bang!" it said. "Shot you dead."

I turned round and saw a man grinning at me.

"Know who I am?" he said. "I'm the butler. Everyone calls me Sid. You can too. You're new, aren't you? Come today, didden you? Want to see my blowgun?"

He showed me a little weapon that fired darts, and demonstrated it by shooting a dart at one of the gateposts. It stuck in the wood quivering, and gave me a decided qualm, as I imagined a similar dart quivering in the flesh of my leg.

"I'd better be getting on," I said hurriedly.

"Okeydoke. Tarra, kid. Be seeing you," Sid said, putting another dart in his gun. "I'm after rabbits. The food they give you here is enough to starve a crow. You'll find *that* out soon enough."

When I had finished dealing with the afternoon post, Miss Vosper, still with the same air of resigned depression, told me that I had better rule up some cards.

"We keep a record of all the pensions ever paid on these pink cards," she said, showing me a whole room full of index drawers, "but with all these cuts in expenditure the ministry aren't issuing any new ones now, so we use up the backs of the old ones when people have died. Rule the lines *exactly* the same as the printed ones on the front, please."

She established me at a table with a pencil, a ruler, and a three-foot-high stack of pink cards. I settled down to work. It wasn't a bad occupation. The cards were, I suppose, six inches by four, and required to have about ten lines on each, the top two lines somewhat spaced apart, so as to take headings in block letters.

Of course I did not reach my full skill in card-ruling in the first few days; that came only after several months, when I had perfected a system of moving the cards along with my elbow, and could dispatch forty a minute, regular as a metronome. The old clerks even unbent to me a little, then, and used to stand round behind me for a few minutes, watching, after the lunch break.

"Quick, isn't she?" they would say to each other, not entirely approving, but not too disparaging, either.

At the end of my first day's work, when the early winter dusk fell and the shutters were drawn, and I was ready to die from strangeness and homesickness, we trooped out of the clerks' room and I discovered that I was to share a bedroom with six of them—Miss Veep, Miss Smarte, Miss Robble, Miss Costard, Miss Whettoe, Miss Clewe. They were all in the room when I went in, washing, changing, and grumbling. Whatever I did, humbly unpacking my belongings, arranging my brush and comb, seemed to be followed by a battery of eyes. They said nothing to me.

Downstairs in one of the wide, icy hallways I was pounced on by Sid.

"Come and get warm in my pantry, kiddo," he said, and took me into a bleak, hot little room full of oilcloth and tin furniture. There he balanced on the fender and looked at me as if I were a great joke. Sid always wore a waiter's suit, black and white, rather soiled. He was balding, hollow-cheeked, handsome in a ravaged, skull-like way, and it didn't take me a moment to fall in love with him. When he began giving me large succulent kisses, though I had never been kissed before in this way and found it remarkable, I nevertheless plunged forward into a new era of experience.

"That's better," said Sid presently, letting go of me and putting us both to rights. "Now you don't look so much like a plucked chicken. Cheez, where do they find 'em?" he said to himself. "Well, reckon I better go and bang the gong. See you some more, kiddo; you and me's going to have fun, I can see that."

He nipped away and banged furiously on a gong the size of King Arthur's round table. As soon as the din began all the lady clerks appeared and glided with decorous frenzy to the dining room. We sat at long tables. All the clerks had their own little pots and jars of condiment ringed around their places like Stonehenge. I noticed that rabbit was on the menu; Sid's hunting had evidently been successful. Sid and a couple of dour maids served us with silent speed; the lady clerks ate with famished, refined rapacity.

"Please God, don't let me wake up in this place," I prayed that night, and for months of nights after. But nevertheless I continued waking up every day to the same existence of cycling through the snow down the hill, pushing the bike back up again, and ruling lines on the pink cards.

After a month I came down with a terrible cold, and Miss Vosper decreed that I was to sit up in the Tower Room, which was less draughty than the little lean-to Post Room where I stuck on the stamps.

The Tower Room occupied the whole top of the tower, and it was filled from side to side with enormously heavy metal filing cabinets, rank behind rank. They stood in grooved runways, and could be shoved sideways, so that access could be obtained to the rear rows. These, of course, held the older and less frequently needed files; if Shakespeare and Chaucer drew pensions, the correspondence about them probably lived here, back in the fourteenth row or thereabouts.

It was warm in the Tower Room, and remarkably quiet; a stray clerk came in very occasionally to put away or take out some ancient letter, but in the main it stayed empty.

Sid popped up sometimes to visit me when I was there; he was not supposed to leave the kitchen quarters but that never worried him.

"Come to the dance tonight, kiddo?" he said one afternoon. "I've got to go into Plymouth after tea. I'll meet you in the village at seven, right?"

I had not even said yes, but of course I would go; I had never been to a dance before, let alone with a butler, but Sid had me under his spell. His cadaverous face, his arms like wishbones, his tremendous fruity kisses like ripe tomatoes were a habit-forming drug.

Seven o'clock found me shivering and sneezing in the

porch of the British Legion hut where the dances were held, in my orange dress, with the bicycle propped against the wall round the corner. Groups of sailors and their girls shoved past; Plymouth was only five miles away.

At a quarter to eight I gave up and went home, primly refusing several offers of drinks from complete strangers. My one aim was to get to bed without encountering Sid (who, I presumed, had forgotten all about his invitation) or incurring questions from Miss Veep, Miss Smarte, Miss Robble or the rest of them. In this I was successful, as they were all at the dance.

Next day I felt rather queer and must have looked it, for Miss Vosper gloomily told one of the other clerks to do my post trips, and I was sent to the Tower Room again. I sat ruling lines, with a feeling like crickets chirping inside my head.

Presently, out of the corner of my eye, I noticed something that had never struck me before: there was a crack of light showing between the long filing-cases. I happened to be sitting half turned away from them, and the light in the corner of my eye began to fidget me; had somebody left a light switched on in the very heart of the metal forest? I stood up and pushed two or three cases to one side or the other—but the overhead lights were all switched off, and I sat down again.

After a while, though, I began, as before, to feel a brightness somewhere over to my left, and, turning quickly, I caught a fierce flash of white light among the cases and saw, far down a corridor of stacks, a little man.

He seemed to be signaling to me.

I was greatly startled, for I had not known that any

other person was in the room, but I slowly threaded my way to him through the stacks, and found that he had clipped one of the working-boards (we called them pastry-boards) onto a shelf, spread out a lot of papers and geometrical instruments on it, and was very busy, like myself, ruling lines.

"Well, me dear," he said, nodding to me in a friendly manner, meanwhile ruling away, much much faster than I could have done. "So you've come up here too, have-ee? Well, make yourself at home, you'm likely to be here a long, long time."

I was feeling strangely drowsy, and leaned against the corner of his shelf, watching the amazing deftness with which he laid dozens of pink cards together and swiftly drew lines across the lot of them.

"You see they meet over there," he said, nodding toward the corner of the room. "Did you know that was infinity, where the lines meet? We're very close to it just here; close—but not quite close enough. It's the speed you work at that makes the difference. I can keep ahead of infinity—if I want to—because I work as fast as light. But I doubt if you can. It's fastness that counts, me dear, fastness every time, in this work."

"But I don't *want* infinity to catch me," I whispered (I was obliged to whisper, because my throat was so sore). "Please tell me how to get away!"

"Well, if you haven't the fastness, you better get inside a circle," he said. "Draw one o' them for yourself—better do it quick. Here's a pair o' compasses."

I took the compasses, fumbling in my haste, and tried to draw a circle, but they slipped and swung and the point stabbed my finger. A tiny bead of blood appeared and, as I stared at it, I suppose infinity caught me.

For a long time I was unconscious, and for a longer time I knew that I was in bed somewhere, but thought, just the same, that I was a captive balloon held on the end of a string by the small man, who, from time to time, gave my string a tweak just to remind me that I now belonged to him. The light round him was unbearably bright and white, and the only way to avoid him was to keep my eyes shut.

After hundreds of hours I opened them and found Sid bringing me a cup of beef tea. He gave me a casual kiss and a grin.

"Hiya, Sleeping Beauty," he said. "Thought you were a goner, we all did. Gave us all a scare, you did."

"What happened to me?"

"Pewmonia, that's all. Here, swaller this and go to by-byes again."

When I was recovered and once more sitting up in the Tower Room I found that spring had come. The darkness that descended like a shutter from teatime to breakfast had lifted; in its place long light evenings drifted by; cuck-oos called.

A new girl had come to do the post, because I had been promoted. The new girl's name was Maize, and she was covered with freckles, had hair like black silk dipped in copper, and eyes bright as blue coals.

Maize feared nothing and nobody; when Miss Vosper treated her to a withering, gloomy, disparaging glare she said loudly, "Yer slip's showing, ducks!" She addressed all

the aged clerks by their first names and never even noticed their outrage; but she referred to them as old cats
when she was with me and wondered how I had stood
them for so long.

Maize could not stick Holm Hall. She wept furious rag-
ing tears as she tried to add the post book—her addition
always came out wrong. The cards she ruled (about three
to the hour) were dirty, crooked, and blotted with misery
and fury. She constantly threatened to run away 'ome, and
only occasionally cheered up when taking long evening
cycle rides with me. We used to drink cider at a couple of
pubs and then whizz down the vertical hills with no
brakes, shrieking and cheering each other on.

Speed had a fascination for me at this time; I knew, or
thought I knew, that my vision of the old man in the
Tower Room had been only a delirious dream, but nevertheless the thought of infinity just around the corner persisted, and I was resolved to keep ahead of it if I could.

The azaleas in the untended garden came out and gar-
landed Holm Hall with their fierce sweet scent. It became
very hot. The Tower Room was hardly tolerable now, but
I still went there to do my work because of the peace and
seclusion and the huge view from its windows down the
summer valley.

One day when I was up there ruling away, quick as
lightning, I saw, far down among the stacks, the same
silvery gleam that I had seen before.

Oh no, I thought in a panic, not again, not now! and I
was making for the door when I heard voices on the stairs.

It was Sid and Maize.

"Is she here?" Sid said. He glanced round the corner

but missed me, standing among the stacks. He had not been up here to see me for a long time.

"No—nobody ain't here," said Maize, and then I saw them move together as if they had been waiting for this moment all their lives; Sid's hands dug deep into her old blue cotton dress; the pair of them fitted like a jigsaw puzzle: in, out, in, out. They stood, a breathing statue, by my empty chair and the scattered pink cards on the pastry-board.

Choking, betrayed, I turned and burrowed among the shelves, for there was no other way out, save past that intense silence.

Light beckoned me, and I made for it.

"Ah," said the old man. "It's you again, is it? In trouble again, are you? Didden you get inside that circle, like I told you?"

"A circle's no use!" I gasped. "Help me, please help me!"

"Now, now," he said, "take it easy. You can't go as fast as all that, not in a panic like you are. That's the wrong kind o' fastness entirely. Look here, now—" He handed me a mirror. "Take a look into that, now."

I gazed, and could not stop gazing. For there was my face, sure enough; but where the eyes should have been I saw nothing but two shining holes, and when I looked through those, it seemed to me that I could see farther and farther in, to an infinite distance.

"Take it easy," the old man said again. "You can see there's naught to worry about."

I was uncertain how to accept this news of the shining, empty universe inside me. I would rather have laid my

151

head down on Sid's shoulder and wept; but that was out of the question; he and Maize had left by the time I came out from among the stacks; and that evening they went off to Liverpool together.

I have never been able to catch up with the old man since that day, but during the course of my long and peaceful life I have often remembered him with gratitude.